"Meri, you must say that I am no unraveled. I am not starving, destitute, or in need of medical care. I am fully aware of my circumstances and live the way I choose. It's not forever, but for now, this is what I must do."

Must do? Why? "See. There you go again, saying nothing, but really? You're piling on the mystery bricks. It's like you're begging me to grill you."

He sighed with exasperation. "And this is exactly why I don't talk to anyone. They only wish to meddle."

"I'm not meddling. I'm curious. For example, are you happy? I mean, living all alone in a dark, wet, cold alley?"

"That is none of your business," he growled.

We pulled up to Shawna's place, and I parked in a guest spot, turning off the engine.

"I'm smelling deflection, which means you're *not* happy. I'm guessing you *could* change things, but you don't want to. You want to suffer. So tell me why, and I'll leave you alone."

"I don't owe you anything." He leaned in close, locking eyes with me. I noticed how his cheekbones curved down toward his upper lip, accentuating their fullness somehow. He really was handsome.

And looking a little pissed off. It was time to back off. "You owe me a win." I hopped out of my red truck. "Coming?"

He grumbled something under his breath and got out. Silently, we made our way to Shawna's townhouse. Once we got to the front door, I rang the bell and turned towards him.

"I'm sorry," I said. "I know I promised not to butt into your life. I'll stop. But if we lose tonight, I'm burning your new tent."

He shook his head at me. "I don't lose."

Strange thing to say for a man in his position, whom some might call a loser. But I was beginning to see he was anything but that. He was tough and stubborn. He was articulate and self-reliant.

So who was Beau Starling?

OTHER WORKS BY MIMI JEAN PAMFILOFF

COMING SOON!
Dragon in Boots (The Immortal Tailor #3) ← Working on it now!
Vampires, Moonshine, and Southern Secrets (Masie Kicklighter #2) ← Woohoo!
Mr. All Out of Love (RevoLUVtion #3) ← He lies. He's full of love.

THE ACCIDENTALLY YOURS SERIES
(Paranormal Romance/Humor)
Accidentally in Love with…a God? (Book 1)
Accidentally Married to…a Vampire? (Book 2)
Sun God Seeks…Surrogate? (Book 3)
Accidentally…Evil? (Novella, Book 3.5)
Vampires Need Not…Apply? (Book 4)
Accidentally…Cimil? (Novella, Book 4.5)
Accidentally…Over? (Book 5, Finale)

THE BOYFRIEND COLLECTOR DUET
(New Adult/Suspense)
The Boyfriend Collector, Part 1
The Boyfriend Collector, Part 2

FANGED LOVE
(Standalone/Paranormal/Humor)

THE FATE BOOK DUET
(New Adult/Humor)
Fate Book
Fate Book Two

THE FUGLY DUET
(Contemporary Romance)
fugly
it's a fugly life

THE HAPPY PANTS SERIES
(Standalones/Romantic Comedy)
The Happy Pants Café (Prequel)
Tailored for Trouble (Book 1)
Leather Pants (Book 2)
Skinny Pants (Book 3)

A HO HO HO BEAU CHRISTMAS, a Standalone Novel
(Romantic Comedy)

IMMORTAL MATCHMAKERS, INC., SERIES
(Standalones/Paranormal/Humor)
The Immortal Matchmakers (Book 1)
Tommaso (Book 2)
God of Wine (Book 3)
The Goddess of Forgetfulness (Book 4)
Colel (Book 5)
Brutus (Book 6)
God of Temptation (Book 7, Finale)

THE IMMORTAL TAILOR SERIES
(Standalones/Paranormal/Dark Humor)
The Immortal Tailor (Book 1)
Vampire in the Jungle (Book 2)
Dragon in Boots (Book 3) ← Coming soon!

THE KING SERIES
(Dark Fantasy/Suspense)
King's (Book 1)
King for a Day (Book 2)
King of Me (Book 3)
Mack (Book 4)
Ten Club (Book 5)
The Dead King (Book 6)
Lord King (Book 7)
Never King's (Book 8, Finale)
Draco (Book 9, Standalone)

THE LIBRARIAN'S VAMPIRE ASSISTANT
(Standalones/Mystery/Humor)
The Librarian's Vampire Assistant (Book 1)
The Librarian's Vampire Assistant (Book 2)
The Librarian's Vampire Assistant (Book 3)
The Librarian's Vampire Assistant (Book 4)
The Librarian's Vampire Assistant (Book 5)
Vampire Man (Book 6, Finale)

MASIE KICKLIGHTER SERIES
Vampires, Whiskey, and Southern Charm (Book 1)
Vampires, Moonshine, and Southern Secrets (Book 2) ← Coming soon!

THE MERMEN TRILOGY
(Dark Fantasy/Suspense)
Mermen (Book 1)
MerMadmen (Book 2)
MerCiless (Book 3)

MR. ROOK'S ISLAND TRILOGY
(Contemporary/Suspense)
Mr. Rook (Book 1)
Pawn (Book 2)
Check (Book 3)

THE OHELLNO SERIES
(Standalones/New Adult/Romantic Comedy)
Smart Tass (Book 1)
Oh Henry (Book 2)
Digging A Hole (Book 3)
Battle of the Bulge (Book 4)
My Pen is Huge (Book 5)
Wine Hard, Baby (Book 6)
Baby, Please (Book 7)
Two Sticky Nuts (Book 8)

REVOLUVTION SERIES
(Romance/Action/Dark Humor)
Mr. Ultra Mega Love (Book 1)
Just Mr. Love (Book 2)
Mr. All Out of Love (Book 3) ← Coming soon!

SUITE #45 SERIES by M.O. MACK
(Thriller/Suspense/Action)
She's Got the Guns (Book 1)

She's Got the Money (Book 2)
She's Got the Time (Book 3)

WALL MEN TRILOGY
(Dark Suspense/Paranormal)
A Haunted House (Book 1)
A Vow Broken (Book 2)
A Promise Kept (Book 3)

WISH, a Standalone Novel
(Romantic Comedy)

A HO HO HO BEAU CHRISTMAS

Mimi Jean Pamfiloff

Copyright © 2024 by Mimi Jean Pamfiloff
Print Edition

All rights reserved. No part of this publication may be reproduced, distributed, or transmitted in any form or by any means, including photocopying, recording, or other electronic or mechanical methods, without the prior written permission of the writer, except in the case of brief quotations embodied in critical reviews and certain other noncommercial uses permitted by copyright law.

This is a work of fiction. Names, characters, places, brands, media, and incidents are either the product of the author's imagination or are used fictitiously. The author acknowledges the trademarked status and trademark owners of various products referenced in this work of fiction, which have been used without permission. The publication/use of these trademarks are not authorized, associated with, or sponsored by the trademark owners.

Editing: Pauline Nolet
Formatting: Paul Salvette
Cover Art: Okay, yes. I did this one myself. It was fun!

DEDICATION

Stefano, I know I threatened to dedicate this sticky sweet holiday treat to you, but really, it's dedicated to Javi, so you're off the hook! (I think *Dragon in Boots* will be yours. Yanno, because you LOVE boots! And fire! #weldersRcool)

Javi, I promised I'd write this book because you said, and I quote, "Why can't you, for once, write a book where the guy isn't some hot, rich dude?"
I dumbly replied, "Sure, honey. Some day. I promise."
Then you added the stipulation that he be a hobo and that it had to be a Christmas story. Then you reminded me repeatedly about my promise.
"Where's my book, lady?"
I think this story satisfies the promise.
Now, please don't ask me for more books!
Hahaha…
Love you.

CHAPTER ONE

"I *love* early Christmas sales," I said to my best friend, Kay, who was shopping with me after our Saturday spin class. "It's like a buffet of orgasms without all the complications of sex."

I grabbed five packages of lights and balanced them atop the giant plastic Santa, red cookie tins, and rolls of foiled wrapping paper in my shopping cart. *Ten percent discount, baby! Woohoo!*

"Oh. I think I just came again." I wiggled my hips. "I just wish my wallet were into it. He's such a frigid bitch."

"Meri, girl," Kay groaned, "you do this every year, and then you're broke for the next twelve months."

Ooh. Santa swizzle sticks! I grabbed three packs.

"Well, yeah," I replied to Kay. "But at least I pay off my credit cards before the next Christmas. Right?" It was how my parents raised me. Always pay your debts, and when it comes to the holidays, give until your eyeballs bleed. And then give a little more.

Okay, okay. That last part wasn't what they

taught me, but they did love Christmas, and growing up, they did such a good job of making the holidays feel magical that I became obsessed. I literally started planning Christmas in January, the moment my dried-out tree went to the curb of my charming, 1920s apartment building with adorable arched windows and stained-glass sidelights. I then started packing up my decorations to go into storage because I wanted to take advantage of the post-holiday clearance sales for the following December.

Well, November, really. Any self-respecting Christmas enthusiast had their lights twinkling, their manger manged, and their fake tree (aka my holiday warmup tree before the live one moved in) re-flocked by mid-November.

Me? I started decorating in October, meaning right about now.

I just loved everything about the season, and it couldn't come fast enough—the smell of fresh cookies and cinnamon candles, the cheery music, the parties and lights and sound of laughter and the miniature reindeer display on my coffee table and my snowflake-shaped dishes and…deep breath, everything!

But most of all, I looked forward to throwing my famous, annual Christmas party. I usually crammed fifty people inside my one-bedroom apartment, but everyone got to experience a magical Christmas and went home with a belly full of decadent treats.

I also gifted everyone in my social circle a tin of my signature sugar cookies. You know, the ones shaped like angels with those little edible pearls and a layer of powdered sugar in a lace pattern—a trick I'd perfected, using a special sifter I'd ordered from France. Set me back fifty dollars, but worth every penny.

"Meri," Kay growled, her big green eyes narrowing on the pile of treasures in my red shopping cart. She only had a bag of apples in hers. *Loser.* "You promised you'd scale back this time so the two of us can take that cruise next summer."

The weighty nuisance of guilt appeared inside my stomach, instantly smothering my pre-holiday shopping buzz. I had promised her, hadn't I?

For the last three years, I'd sworn up and down that we'd go, but every time she went to book time off from work, I'd tell her I didn't have the money.

She'd gotten so desperate last spring that she'd offered to pay my way—three thousand dollars for a two-week cruise in the Caribbean. First-class cabin with a balcony, endless views of turquoise water, and five-star dining. It was a high nail on her bucket list, right up there with marrying a man who loved to cook gourmet dinners and give three-hour-long foot rubs.

Of course, I'd turned down her generous offer to pay my way, feeling ashamed of myself for being so broke. Again.

But honestly? She worked just as hard as I did,

and I wasn't about to mooch. She was in real estate, and I was an insurance analyst who specialized in insuring big developers. Yes, I made decent money, but it somehow ended up under the tree each year.

Anyway, after I said no thank you in the nicest possible way, Kay cried and declared she'd go without me next summer. I felt like garbage and swore up and down I would *not* be broke next year. I would save, and we'd go together.

But, gah! I love Christmas. I eyed the stuff in my cart and then looked at Kay's crinkled lips preparing to unleash some choice words. She fully expected me to break another promise, and she'd be right.

Could I really do this to her—choose an amazing Christmas over Kay? We'd been best friends since middle school, ever since Kevin Foster started making fun of my freckles and frizzy brown curls. Every day he'd come up with a new name for me—fuzz butt, pork rind, rat's nest, and pube head. Then one day, he'd called me "slutty tumbleweed," claiming I just rolled from guy to guy like a "wild bag of hoes." He added that each freckle on my face was a devil's kiss for all the boys I'd banged. "Marks of shame," he'd called them. I guessed his parents were super religious or something, and he'd improvised on their teachings.

Well, my parents were religious, too—super Catholics—which was why I knew he'd missed some major points about kindness. His words were truly cruel and most definitely intended for everyone to hear, which was why the other boys in class, and even some of the girls, had laughed.

The only one who stuck up for me was Kay, and though I'd gained a best friend that day—something I was eternally grateful for—the damage was done. From that day forward, I got the illegitimate reputation for being a ho bag. A slut. An easy score. My D-cups didn't help defuse the situation either, so I also gained a phobia.

I was so terrified of even looking at a boy and being accused of sluttism that I didn't have my first real relationship until college.

After a year, my ex and I broke up because he said I was uptight and way too concerned about what other people thought. Also, he hated Christmas. Was never going to work out.

The strange part was, my last boyfriend, Mike, loved Christmas, but he'd said the same thing: I was too self-conscious. But who wouldn't be after what I'd gone through in high school? The boys wanted to date me for all the wrong reasons, and the girls hated me for getting attention. Kay and a handful of other friends kept me sane through it all.

I was twenty-nine now—on the precipice of thirty—and I'd be single for the holidays again. If it weren't for Kay and her unwavering friendship, I'd probably just give up on romance and marry a cucumber.

"You're right," I said and drew a deep, fortifying breath. What I was about to say next would not sit well with the hungry holiday monster inside. "I made a promise, and this year, I'm keeping it."

Kay glanced at the stuff in my cart and folded her toned arms over her flat chest. "Then put it all back."

I arched a brow. *This stuff is ten percent off!*

"I'm serious, Meri. Put it back. If you're keeping your promise—which you'd better—then you won't spend a dime on Christmas this year."

"I said I'd scale back. And I will. But I still *have* to decorate for my party."

"Then let everyone chip in for the food," she suggested. "I'll bake a big cake."

"I can't invite people over and then ask them to bring their own food." How tacky. Plus, my food was always special and went with a theme.

"You can if you throw a potluck," she argued.

I gave her a dirty look.

"Okay, then at least use the stuff in your storage locker. You'll save a ton of money on decorations." She grabbed the plastic Santa from my cart, sending the packages of lights tumbling to the floor.

Oh no! They'll never twinkle now.

She went on, "And don't even start, because I know for a fact that you have five of these Santas already."

I went in for St. Nick, reclaiming him from her hands. "The red paint fades. I always get a new one. He deserves to look his best."

She took back plastic Santa. "Then buy a two-dollar tube of red paint from the craft section and give the man a new coat. Saves you forty-eight dollars."

Maybe she had a point. Also, my storage unit was getting pretty full. I hoarded everything from prior Christmases for when I finally bought a house. I mean, how else would I decorate a five-bedroom, four-bath, two-story country home with a red barn on five snowy acres without having lots and lots of Santas? The way I saw it, I was investing in my future.

Still, maybe I could scale back just once. *For Kay. For the cruise.*

"Okay," I said, "but I still have to wrap presents."

"Dollar store."

I gasped. "You know I only use gold- or red-foiled paper. The lights on the tree make the presents sparkle. Dollar store doesn't carry that stuff."

"Well, you'll just have to make do since that's where you're doing your shopping this year for gifts."

A wave of nausea climbed up my throat. Not that I had anything against shopping there, but I already had handmade crafts picked out for everyone. I loved supporting the artists, the crafters, and the wood carvers of the world. I made sure that everyone on my list got a totally unique—and, yes, sometimes expensive—item to add to their own decorations.

Last year, I ordered reindeer sculptures from Norway, inscribed with each person's name. Set me back one hundred dollars per person. With forty people on my list—parents, my two older brothers, their wives, my six nieces and nephews, my five aunts and uncles, ten cousins, and my closest friends—well, you do the math. That didn't include the cost of my party, decorations, or masterful cookie gifts. I also made little gift bags for about twenty people at work. Nothing fancy. Just a cute ornament for their trees plus a custom-printed card of me.

In front of last year's tree. Alone. But I was hopeful that would change. In the meantime, I had…*Christmas to keep me happy!*

"Are you really doing this to me?" I whined. "You're taking away my Christmas?"

Her green eyes filled with rage. "You know what?" She grabbed the Santa and slammed it down inside my cart. "I give up." She took her cart and started rolling away.

"You don't see me telling you not to buy your stupid hair dye, do you?" Kay was a natural blonde, but loved coloring her hair the exact same shade every three weeks for uniformity purposes. She was a perfectionist when it came to her looks. Not an ounce of unneeded fat on her body or a flabby anything. I was pretty flexible when it came to all that, except for managing my frizz. I straightened my brown hair most days or wore it in a bun. "And *you're* obsessed with your butt! That's why it's so tight. Tight ass!"

"Take me off your list!" she yelled after she turned the corner. "We are not best friends anymore."

My mouth dropped. "Fine with me, you holiday hate…er…" My words faded with a sad little sigh. I knew she was right to be upset. She'd put up with me and my Christmas mania for far too long.

I just…I just couldn't stand the thought of throwing anything but a spectacular holiday party or the idea of giving out presents that didn't say, "I put a lot of time and effort into your gift." It was an essential element to making everyone feel special.

But Kay *neve*r asked for anything. Well, except to borrow my red truck every once in a while when she moved. But aside from that, she only asked for friendship, and here I was shattering her dream of the two of us cruising around in the tropics.

I looked at the items in my cart. "Sorry, guys, but it's you or Kay."

CHAPTER TWO

That night, I texted Kay with a heartfelt apology and a photo of my final shopping cart containing only milk, yogurt, and some oranges.

She texted back saying that she would accept my apology if, and only if, I stuck to my promise of spending next to nothing on Christmas and saving my money for that cruise. I couldn't blame her for doubting my resolve. I'd proven I couldn't help myself when the holidays rolled around.

This year would be different.

I spent Sunday doing laundry and making a list of gifts under five dollars. Next weekend, I'd make a trip to my storage locker. With a little planning, I could make good use of my older decorations and salvage my party. I just hated throwing all my plans out the window and starting from scratch like this. I was slammed at work and had very little free time as it was.

Monday evening, after a long day at the office, I pulled up to the back alley of my apartment building to park my truck inside for the night. I generally didn't like using the tiny, narrow garage underneath the building because it was a tight squeeze, but the forecast said we'd be getting snow tonight, and I hated cleaning my windshield in the morning. Took forever.

I pulled in, angling the nose of my red truck toward my garage door, which had to be opened by hand. Like I'd said, it was an old building, so the ceilings were too low for a garage door opener and a truck.

I was about to hop out but noticed a bright red tent next to the dumpster beside my garage door. There was a little light on inside.

Someone was camping there. *What the...?* Not only was it illegal to pitch a tent on private property, but I was a single woman who knew the dangers of living in the city. The rent here might be expensive, and the neighborhood might be filled with nice old homes, but that didn't mean it was safe to just walk around by yourself at night in dark alleys. It certainly wasn't safe to have strangers just living on your doorstep. Or garage door step. Whatever. The point was, clearly some crazy person was inside that tent because it was way too cold to live outside.

I backed up and headed out of the alley. I'd have to park out front on the street.

Twenty minutes later, I was knocking on my downstairs neighbor's door, feeling beyond annoyed after walking four blocks in the freezing wind to get to our building because there were no spots nearby.

"Jason!" I knocked again, my teeth chattering in the hallway. Jason, a divorced dad in his forties with thinning brown hair and lots of tattoos, was basically the building's manager, getting a steep discount on rent in exchange for doing repairs and keeping an eye on things. Next door to him was Mrs. Trudy, an unfriendly woman in her seventies, and upstairs, next to me, was Mrs. Larson, a retired teacher in her sixties. She was nice, but left her TV on too loud.

I heard the clicking of the deadbolt, and the door opened.

"Hey, Jason," I said, still shivering despite being indoors. "Sorry to bother you."

He wiped his mouth with the napkin in his hand, swallowing down whatever he was eating. "Just having dinner. What's up?"

"What's up? Did you know," I lowered my voice, "there's a crazy person camped out by the dumpster?"

He frowned. "Crazy person?"

"Yeah. I mean, they'd have to be to sleep outside in this weather. They should be in a shelter or something. They'll freeze to death."

He nodded slowly. "Yes, it's going to be cold tonight."

I went on, "And honestly, Jason, I don't feel comfortable being all alone back there at night to begin with. Now I have to deal with homeless people camping right next to my garage? Next, I won't be able to toss my trash without having to jump over piles of poop or dirty needles. They can't live there."

He gave me a look, like I was being a little cruel.

"Oh, come on, Jason. You know I'm sympathetic—the world isn't an easy place—but women have to protect themselves. You have a daughter. You know what I mean. Homeless encampments aren't safe for anyone."

He looked down at the ground for a second, like he was in no mood for this conversation. "I understand your concern about strangers living in the alleyway, but I already talked to the guy, and I promise you, he's harmless. He said he's only staying for a few days, and then he's moving on. So no encampment."

"You knew about him sleeping there? And you didn't do anything?" I snapped.

I wondered why the other tenants and our neighbors weren't making a stink. The people on our block were way more uptight than me. Mostly because they were older and grew up in this neighborhood. That somehow turned them into guard dogs. They were constantly spying on everyone and had the cops on speed dial. You couldn't throw so much as a gum wrapper on the sidewalk—not that I would, because litter bugs. Blech!—without hearing about it.

"Meri, there's nothing to worry about, okay?

Just pretend he's not there, and he'll be gone by next weekend."

I narrowed my eyes. It was one thing to be sympathetic, but having a vagrant camp on our property wasn't the solution. He needed to be where he could get access to resources, food, warmth, and, well, a bathroom. "I'm calling the owners."

Jason shook his head. "Be my guest, but by the time they do anything, he'll be gone."

I couldn't believe this. "So I'm just going to have to deal with a man going to the bathroom all over the place, dumping his trash everywhere?"

"He's been there for two nights already. Did you see any of that?"

"Well, no."

"Then?" Jason raised a brow.

"That's not the point. How am I supposed to use the garage with some strange man right there? What if he attacks me?"

Jason sighed. "I need to go. My food's getting cold. But trust me when I tell you he's not going to bother you. He doesn't do drugs or drink. He's just…different is all."

"Camping in the cold isn't *different*. It's suicidal. I'm going to sue if I come home to a popsicle man back there. PTSDD—popsicle trauma syndrome over dead dude."

"Good night, Meri." Jason closed the door.

"Wha-what?" I felt like the world was going mad. Being compassionate didn't mean giving up your own rights or safety. It didn't mean letting people break the law and live wherever they liked.

"You'd better be right," I yelled through the door. "He needs to be gone by next weekend, or I'm calling the cops."

I huffed and went to my apartment to defrost.

CHAPTER THREE

"Seriously? You're siding with Jason?" I said to Kay later in the week as we both virtually climbed our way to Mount Everest from the warmth and safety of stair machines in the gym. We tried to meet up here three times a week after work. Kay took her workouts seriously, which kept me honest. There was no slacking on her watch.

"Of course I'm siding with Jason." Panting, Kay shrugged. "It's a city."

"What's that supposed to mean?" I huffed out my words with ten minutes left in my workout. *God, please help me finish. This is brutal.* But I'd eaten a box of Twinkies for lunch, so now it was time to pay up.

"In a city," she replied, "you get access to incredible restaurants, art, culture, and vibes, but with it comes crime, gross smells, weirdos, too much traffic, and the homeless. It's part of the deal."

"The guy is literally a foot from my garage, and I have to get out of my truck to open it, not to mention, I have to walk all the way to the back stairs to get inside." Our building didn't have direct access to the garages, which were four separate spaces. You had to use the concrete stairs that ran between our building and the building next door. At the bottom of the stairs was a steel gate leading to the alley.

"You're *always* complaining about your apartment building. So move."

"Pfft! To a new skyrise condo like yours?" No character. No charm. Just lots of stainless steel, elevators, and shiny new tile. I loved older buildings. They had personality that made the neighborhood unique.

"You'd probably save four or five hundred a month," she pointed out. "Plus, secure underground parking and a security guard."

"No thanks." Though, I might have to consider moving soon if the owners—some big company—raised the rent again. If it weren't for the place being one block from my favorite coffee shop and Christmas boutique, plus a short commute to work, which I did by bus when the weather wasn't a ball-freezer, I would have moved already.

"Meri, I can get you a rental in my building. My company manages the property. You just need a steady job and good credit, which we both know you have."

Good job, *perfect* credit. Never missed a payment.

She added, "Just say the word, and I'll find you a place. Even an old crappy one like you have now."

"Hey," I protested, "just because something's

old doesn't make it crappy. But thank you."

"What are friends for? Especially if it helps you get to the finish line faster. *If* you get there."

She meant that she still didn't believe I'd keep my word about not spending myself into the poorhouse for Christmas. Even though we were talking again, things were still tense between us, almost like Kay was pre-angry and fully expected to be let down again. *Guilty until proven innocent.*

"I'll get there," I said. "In fact, I'm going to my storage unit this weekend to sort through all of my stuff. Want to come?"

"Can't. Going to hang out with my sister. She's pregnant."

"Again?" I said.

"Yep. Number four."

"Jesus. She's a year younger than us." I started pumping my legs faster on the stair machine, making my large tatas bounce all over the place.

"I know, but why are you doing that?" Her eyes darted to my feet and then to my chest. "Jeez. Go easy on the girls, Meri. They might fall off."

"I'm getting oxygen to my ovaries. It could be a while until I put them to use." I didn't even have a boyfriend.

She laughed. "Not sure it works that way, but the exercise can't hurt since cookie season is coming." She paused. "Oh, by the way, I started seeing someone."

I stopped climbing.

"Guy from work," she added.

My jaw dropped. "Coffee guy?"

She smiled. "He's dinner guy now. Also breakfast. Two times."

My eyes went wide. "Ohmygod. That's great. Why didn't you tell me?" She'd been pining for him for months, trying to work up the courage to tell him she was interested without it getting awkward. Dating at work wasn't easy these days. Lots of HR landmines. But how else were people our age supposed to meet other dysfunctional, horny, semi-responsible adults to settle down with?

"I didn't want to jinx it, but he's...wonderful." Her cheeks began glowing to a rosy, smitten shine. "I even let him go down on me."

The guy on the stair machine next to her looked over and grinned, giving a nod of approval.

"Mind your business, perv," I barked and then looked at Kay. "Big step. I'm proud of you." Like me, she had her hang-ups. Hers were mostly rooted to the fact her parents refused to let her have a phone, razor, or makeup until she was eighteen. Super-hippies. She'd never even tried meat until she was thirteen. My ham sandwich. Anyway, I helped her defy them any chance I got, as a good teenager and best friend should, but there wasn't much I could do about her razor situation. I gave her one every time my mom bought me a pack, but she had to decide when to use them. Summertime was always the worst for her because her parents would know if she'd shaved since we spent lots of time at the pool. Unfortunately, her first boyfriend, at the age of sixteen, discovered the hard way what she had going on down there. Seventies bush. Wild, unfettered, womanly jungle meant only for the most seasoned explorer.

He had *not* come armed with a machete.

Nor had he been prepared for a mouthful of bristly foliage.

Yet the fool had gone diving in with an open mouth, like an eager child attacking an ice-cream cone. What happened next was a nightmare of gagging and coughing since he'd apparently inhaled a curlicue. Kay never recovered from the event, even if she'd taken control of her life after high school. The woman had a punch card for Brazilian waxes.

"So, was it good?" I asked, snapping my eyes toward the interloper next to us, who was now pretending not to listen.

"It was better than good." She leaned toward me. "In fact, he asked me to, you know, grow it out a little, and I did."

"What? Wow, Kay! You have a baby bush now?"

Proudly, she nodded. "I do. I mean, it's just a landing strip—for, like, a small Cessna—two prop max, but he's super into it. And honestly, I'm liking the break from the pain."

I'd bet. "So when do I get to meet him?"

"I dunno. It's all still new. Maybe give us a week

or four months?"

Huh? "Kay, I have to meet him."

She looked away.

"What?" I knew her, and this was a clear sign that she didn't want to say something. "You can tell me anything. You know that, right?"

She groaned. "He's a Buddhist."

Buddhist? "And?"

"Well, he doesn't celebrate Christmas, Meri."

Holy crap. Was my best friend telling me that she didn't think I'd get along with a person, her *possible* future person, because he wasn't into Christmas?

"Kay, how can you say that? You know me. I mean, yes, I loooove Christmas, but I'm not going to shun the man of your dreams if he's anti-Santa or not a Jesus groupie." *Like my parents.* I mean, how many crucifixes did one house need? Last time I'd counted, they had eighty-three Jesuses on the cross pegged to the living room wall. Blue-eyed Jesus, bleeding Jesus, angelic Jesus, Black Jesus, and my personal favorite, Latin lover Jesus with the tan and amazing six-pack. They had every flavor imaginable.

"You sure about that?" Kay asked.

"Yes, I'm sure. Why?" I asked.

"Mike," she said.

My latest ex? "What about him? He loved Christmas."

"No. He *liked* Christmas. Like a normal person. But the moment he told you that he wanted to spend the holidays in Canada with his parents, who only celebrate with a simple family dinner, you started talking yourself out of being with him."

"Not true. He dumped me because he said I was too uptight," I argued.

"Exactly. You're so obsessed with Christmas that you've literally forgotten the entire point."

"Oh, shut up, Miss Bah Hum Booger. I get the point just fine."

"And yet," she said, "I'm terrified that you'll try to talk me out of dating Lick. The moment you two meet, you'll start gushing over your party plans, and you'll brag about your decorations."

"Hold on. Back up. His name is Lick? And he went down on you?" I bit the inside of my cheeks, trying not to laugh.

"See! This is why I didn't want to introduce you," she snapped. "And for the record, Leonardo is his real name. Lick is some family nickname."

Did I want to know why? Yes, yes, I did. But that could wait. "So you were afraid I'd tease your new man, Lickasaurus?"

She gave me a hateful look. "I *know* you'll tease him. And then scare him off with your psychotic relationship with the month of December."

"I won't deny my addiction, but I don't see why that concerns him?"

"He won't share your enthusiasm, and you'll feel like it's a slap. Then you'll be calling him a hater."

I gasped. "No, I won't."

"Meri, it's time someone told you the truth." She got down from her machine and stepped closer to me, lowering her voice. "It's one thing to want to celebrate your special day, but you have to stop *obsessing* over Christmas. And before you accuse *me* of being a hater, let me clarify: Christmas is not about parties, decorations, or gifts, it's about opening your heart to others. It's a feeling, not a thing. And the only way to feel it is by giving from the heart. Not material things, but heart things. Actual kindness from the soul."

"I've gone to five weddings and eight baby showers in twelve months." Everyone I knew seemed to be getting married or starting families. "Do you have any idea how many gifts that is? All I do is give, give, give from the heart all year round." Why was she saying such ugly crap to me? *Hater.*

"You *are* a generous person, but during the holidays, the merry Meri monster takes over. You try to mesmerize everyone with your elaborate decorations and wow them with the expense of it all. But if you really wanted to give, you'd do it without expecting anything in return, including validation."

I felt like Kay had holiday punched me in the chimney chute. Sure, I liked receiving compliments about my masterful decorating skills, but I didn't *need* validation. My deep love of Christmas was what drove me. And I couldn't believe she didn't want me to meet her non-Christmassy boyfriend.

"I swear to you," I said, "if you introduce me to Lick, I won't even mention the word Christmas, okay? Why don't you guys come over for dinner after you get back from seeing your sister? I'll make lasagna. He can eat that, right?"

She gave me a look.

"What? I don't know if he's, like, a super-vegetarian Buddhist or one of those holiday-only religious people like me." My parents were super Catholics, but I pretty much phoned it in all year except for major holidays. Drove my mom crazy. But I figured that God made me church lazy, so he didn't mind.

"I think it might be better if we find neutral ground—ease him into the world of Meri since you'll already have your decorations up."

"Whatever you think's best." I smiled contentedly, ready to prove myself. I could let go of Christmas and act like a normal person who enjoyed the holidays but whose life didn't revolve around them.

Couldn't I?

"Oh," Kay added, "you can meet him at Friendsgiving. You're coming, right?"

She held it every year on Thanksgiving since neither of us went to our parents' until Christmas. Our town was a five-hour drive in the mountains if the weather was good.

"I wouldn't miss it," I replied.

"But you know the rules, Meri. You have to

bring a plus one."

"No…" I whined. "This again?" She knew I wasn't seeing anyone.

"It's tradition. We all have to bring a person who's flying solo for Turkey Day."

It was a nice tradition, but I hated the task of asking around the office or texting my level-two friends—aka "good friends" but not *best* friend—to see if anyone would come with me. "Fine. I'll figure it out."

"That's my girl," she said. "Now move your ass. You still have five minutes to go on the machine to burn off whatever crap you ate for lunch. It was a Twinkie, wasn't it? I can see the guilt on your hips."

More like twelve Twinkies, but who was counting?

CHAPTER FOUR

I spent all day Saturday combing through my storage unit for decorations I could rework into a new theme that felt fresh and cheerful, which turned out to be less of a challenge than I'd thought.

Every year, I put out a few classic pieces—like the light-up Santa for my nonworking fireplace—but then I came up with a unique theme so each party would be memorable.

Last year, the theme was "winter palace" complete with glowing icicles and light-up igloo bricks stacked up around the inside of my front door so when someone entered my apartment, it was like walking out of an igloo and into a Christmas wonderland. I covered all of my furniture in white and had several snowflake lightshows staged around the apartment. The year before that, I did a gingerbread-house theme. The inside of my apartment was like being inside a colorful graham-cracker castle—basically a thousand cookies glued to sheets, which I hung on the walls and decorated with frosting. A triumph!

Honestly, I'd had so much fun reliving years of

holiday decorating that I didn't want to put everything away again. Especially the items I'd made by hand like my Christmas tree appetizer tower with tiny red-and-white saucers glued to each branch so my guests could pick a snack in the shape of little presents. The phyllo dough boxes stuffed with herbed feta and little sundried tomato chunks that looked like red bows came out great.

Anyway, since I was on a budget and loving this walk down memory lane, I decided to select the best pieces and name this year's theme "walk down Christmas lane." It was the perfect way to remind my friends of all the fun they'd had in prior years.

The only downside to my brilliant plan was that I had to get all of my crap from my truck into my apartment, and some of the boxes weighed a ton. I'd need to unload everything into my garage, unpack the boxes, and move the items a little at a time.

I pulled up to my private garage and immediately spotted the red tent. *Why's he still here?* Well, I'd just have to take Jason's word that the man was harmless.

I parallel parked, careful not to get my front bumper too close to the tent, and then hopped out to unlocked the garage door. As I lifted, the whole thing groaned and creaked like old bones bending under the weight of time.

I went to my tailgate and began carefully sliding out the box of candy-cane-painted plates.

"Oh no!" The tape on the bottom was coming

apart, the gap between the flaps separating under my hands. *Shit. Shit!* I was about to push the box back into the truck bed when I heard a deep voice to my side.

"Let me help," he said.

I turned my head to find a man with bright blue eyes and a scraggly black beard reaching for my box. Before I could tell him no, he snatched the box from my hands, and the contents dumped out. Right on his feet.

"Son of a snowman!" The man howled in pain.

I looked down and noticed that he didn't seem to be wearing shoes. Kind of crazy given the cold weather.

"Why didn't you warn me how heavy that was!" he yelled.

My mouth flapped for a moment. "Well, I-I didn't have time and…"

His eyes began tearing up.

"Oh, God." I carefully began moving the broken plates off his feet, and that's when I noticed a chunk of China sticking from the top of his left foot. "Okay. You're hurt. You're hurt. Ummm…I'll take you to the ER."

"No. I'm fine."

I arched a brow. He had a two-inch-long triangle with half a candy cane lodged in his flesh. "Let me take you upstairs to clean it."

Was I really inviting a stranger into my apartment? That wasn't smart. On the other hand, what choice did I have? He was bleeding. The least I could do was clean the wound and send him on his way.

"No. Thank you. I have a first aid kit in my tent," he said coldly.

I blinked, realizing who this was. *Tent Man.*

He added sternly, "And you shouldn't invite strange men into your home. It's not safe. All sorts of crazy people out there."

He was right, but did he have to sound like such a dick about it? "Thank you for saving me from serial killers like you. Phew! That was a close one."

"What gave me away?" he said dryly, clearly taking insult.

"The splash of psycho in your eyes," I said, not at all serious, but if he wanted to play this game of down-talk, then fine. "*And* you came to my rescue when I didn't ask, which means you wanted to impress me, possibly lure me into your white van. Also, you're not wearing shoes, unless you count my peppermint paradise limited-edition holiday plate sticking out of your foot."

"Definitely not a shoe." He winced in pain.

Oh no. Poor guy. "Hey, you're bleeding. Let me bring you some warm water and soap."

"Thanks, but I don't need help."

"And I didn't need yours, but here I am with a box full of irreplaceable broken dishes thanks to you." Honestly, I'd had everything under control.

"What I meant to say is that if I did need help, I

wouldn't ask you." He turned and began hobbling away, disappearing inside his red tent.

Good. Go hide in your portable gremlin cave. Jerk. I closed my tailgate and started my engine, deciding to call it a day. I parked my truck inside with all of the stuff in the back. Then I got to cleaning up all the broken dishes.

Tomorrow, I'd see if Jason was around and could help unload some stuff. Maybe Kay would be back from her sister's and help, too.

The good news was Jason had been right. Tent Man wasn't the rapey type that I could tell, but he sure was a rude butthole.

෴ ෴

"Can you believe this tent guy?" I griped on Monday to my coworker and friend Shawna, who sat in the cubicle next to mine. She was one of the only people my age in the office who was single and not doing the domestic-bliss thing. In other words, she could relate to my dating-app horror stories or occasional spontaneous bawling.

No, I didn't cry because I was single. Not exactly. I cried during certain times of the month when I felt, well, horny. Maybe I was ovulating or something. But there was something inherently deflating about knowing you were going home to the massage head on your shower, a bright purple banana-shaped thing, or your manual bean flicker when what you really wanted was a man who knew you—your body, your smile, your favorite Christmas song—along with knowing just how to move inside you to ignite a fire so hot, so forceful, that your head exploded like a pumpkin tossed from a two-story window. So yeah, once a month, I wept for my empty bed and for my lonely bean. I wept because I knew he was out there somewhere, and if I'd just made different choices in life, I probably would've found him by now. Instead, I'd wasted my time with men like Mike.

Shawna, who had long black braids, deep brown skin, and the sharpest tongue I'd ever met, gave me a shrug.

"A shrug? From you?" I said. "Where's the quippy, colorful language, telling me to go fuck my own asshole? Or, your personal favorite, an ad hoc limerick about whiny bitches?"

She shrugged again.

"Shawna, what the hell? You never hold back."

She grabbed her sports drink bottle and started guzzling as if stalling for time.

"Shawna!" I hissed.

She stopped drinking. "Fine. I think you should apologize to the guy."

To Tent Man? "For what? All I did was offer help." After he'd broken my dishes.

"You obviously did something to offend the guy, and let's get real, Meri: you're not the most self-aware person in the world."

I blinked, allowing that to soak in. So Mike said I was uptight, Kay thought I was superficial in my holiday ways, and now Shawna was telling me I wasn't self-aware? "You really think that?"

She shrugged again. That was three shrugs in one conversation. And not one snappy talk-down. Shawna was serious.

"I, uh…thank you for letting me know," I said, feeling deflated. And shunned. It wasn't as if the feedback was coming from some rando on social media who didn't know me.

Fuck. I'd always thought I was a giver. A kind person. A thoughtful person. Maybe I wasn't.

I sank into my computer chair and stared at my monitor.

"Hey," said Shawna, leaning over the divider, "you okay? I didn't mean to upset you or anything."

"No, it's okay," I muttered. "I'll just go kill myself now. Maybe a sharp knife or poison."

She said nothing, so I turned my head and found a worried-looking Shawna.

"I was joking," I snapped.

"Not funny." She shook her head at me.

"I really appreciate your honesty. Maybe it's what I needed to hear." Because the truth was, I did care about people. *My* people. My family, friends, neighbors, and coworkers. I cared about my community. But what good was any of that if they weren't feeling it?

To be clear, I'd always thought that my big holiday bash was "Appreciation Month for Everyone in Meri's Life." It was why I went all out. But maybe that was where I'd been going wrong. I'd been appreciating them my way. I'd been celebrating *my* favorite holiday, thinking *my* gift was sharing *my* passion with them.

"Maybe I just live in a bubble," I muttered. "The Meri bubble."

"Honestly? I think it's that you're always worried about making people happy. You act like you owe everyone something. For example, you don't need to bake me muffins every week or bring me lattes all the time. Yes, I appreciate them, but it makes me feel guilty. I don't know why, but it does. And when I tell you not to do it, you do it anyway."

"I do it because I owe *you* for being the only person at work I can talk to." Just like I owed Kay for putting up with the constant cruise ship letdowns. I owed everyone I loved.

Shawna gave me a hard look. "Do you see me running around like I owe you anything?"

I shook my head.

"Exactly. We've been friends for five years. We've helped each other through hangover workdays, bad bosses, and the occasional creepy coworker. I'm here for you, Meri. I have your back, and you have mine. That's enough for me."

I smiled shallowly. "It's enough for me, too."

"Good. Then stop acting like my friendship is a membership that needs to be renewed all the time.

You already paid up by being a wonderful human being and by being there when I need you."

She was right. I always felt friendships were like plants that required constant watering. But maybe they were more like works of fine art you had to display in a place of honor in your heart, where they could be appreciated.

"Thanks, Shawna. You really are a great friend."

"I am, which is why I'm also going to add that I still want holiday cookies and an invite to your party."

My mood instantly elevated. "You don't think they're too much?"

"Hell no. I love your psycho-bitch, Christmas spazzfest. It's like Hannibal Lecter and Santa had a baby who feeds on reindeer's nutsacks and jizz-flavored eggnog. So sick. Yet I can't stop wanting more."

I smiled big. *There she is, my Shawna.* "Have I ever told you how much I fucking love your gross shit-talk? Magical. Also, I think I have to throw up now."

"Jizz nog too much for you?"

"Stop." I covered my mouth.

"How about sack nog? Or sweaty Santa foreskin sippy juice?"

"Enough. Please." I held up my palm. "I'm going to throw up in my mouth. By the way, what do you want for lunch?"

"Oddly, I'm craving clam chowder," she said

flatly.

"Me too. Meet you out front in a sec. I need to make a quick call." I grabbed my purse and headed out.

Once outside, I quickly dialed Jason, but it went to voicemail. "Hey, it's Meri. I'm really sorry about not trusting you before. I mean, yeah, you work for our landlord, so that kind of makes you an insta-dick, but you were right about the camper. He seems okay. So can you do me a favor if he's still there? Tell him I'm an okay person, too. Tell him I appreciate how he came to my rescue and that all I wanted was to make sure he doesn't die of an infection. I just…wanted him to know in case he decides to take off today. Thanks, bye."

I hung up, hoping I'd at least make one thing right. Not that I was entirely sure what I'd done wrong.

CHAPTER FIVE

That evening, despite the new snowstorm rolling in, I parked my red truck out front of my building since my garage was partially filled with boxes. Hopefully the weather would clear by Friday because this weekend was the big kickoff. I would carry up my decorations, lock myself away from the world, play my favorite holiday songs, and drink white peppermint-tinis until I puked. But so help me God, I would not leave my apartment until I'd transformed it into a magical oasis of Christmas cheer.

I got to my place and shed my red coat, snow boots, and white crocheted hat, leaving everything to dry on my reindeer bench complete with faux antlers for hanging one's coat. It was a very special find, hand-carved in Greenland by a little old man who spent his days looking out the window at actual reindeer. I wanted to go there one day. I'd read about a spa with cabins made of thermal glass so you could see in every direction for tens of miles. They said if you were lucky, you'd catch a glimpse of the aurora borealis. If you were super lucky, you just might see a plump old man shooting across the sky in a sleigh, carrying a load of supplies as he prepared for the big day.

Not that I actually believed in Santa. I was a grown woman. But I still got into the holiday spirit and sent a letter to him each year. It was fun. Also, maybe a bit cathartic. For example, last year I asked for bigger hearts for everyone in the world who seemed to not care anymore. Then I asked for clarity regarding my relationship with Mike.

"If he's not the one, Santa, just move him out and move Mr. Right in. I'm tired of taking my annual holiday photo alone in front of my tree, even if I am incredibly grateful for my family and friends. No complaints there! But it's starting to feel like something's missing during the holidays."

I also added that if he couldn't help with any of those things, I'd settle for a trip to that spa in Greenland. How fun to sip hot cocoa on a cold winter night and watch the stars near the North Pole.

Some day. First, though, I had a tropical cruise to do.

I cracked open a can of noodle soup and popped the bowl in the microwave while I changed into my flannel PJs. As I sat looking over my list of to-dos for the weekend, my mind started wandering to the alleyway.

Was Tent Man still there? Had Jason passed along my message? I got up and peeked out my living room window, catching a glimpse of the corner of a red tent.

"Seriously?" It was a snowy hell out there.

Honestly, I didn't know why, but I felt…annoyed. Genuinely, thoroughly annoyed. Where did he get off freezing to death next to my garage?

Maybe he's dead already.

I slid on my boots and red coat and grabbed my keys, ready to unleash some winter safety tips. But the moment I stepped outside, my irritation turned to genuine concern. In the last forty minutes, the temperature had dropped another fifteen degrees. Yes, I had a built-in thermometer called nipples. They weren't just rock hard, they were asking for mercy.

Wind gusting, snowflakes pelting my eyeballs—so unpleasant—I fought my way down the slippery concrete stairs to the gate and out to the alley.

I marched through what was now five inches of snow toward the red tent. A dim light was on inside. "Hey, Tent Man! You in there?"

I didn't hear a reply, but I wasn't exactly expecting him to welcome me after our last interaction.

"Hey. You need to go somewhere warm," I yelled. "You'll literally die out here, and the last thing I need is to think of some dead guy who froze during a nasty storm every time I take out the trash. So get your ass out of there, okay? I'll drive you anywhere you need to go."

Silence.

"Tent guy?"

Silence.

My heart started pounding while booger-cicles formed on the end of my freezing nose.

"Fuck this." I bent down and unzipped the tent's opening. I poked my head inside to find the man lying motionless under a blanket. I gave his foot a squeeze, but he didn't react.

"Oh no." I crawled inside and started shaking him. "Hey! Wake up. Can you hear me?" He was still breathing, but his skin was cold. "You need to open your eyes. Wake up!" I smacked his bearded cheek, but nothing.

Christ, he's dying. And unfortunately, I'd left my cell in my apartment.

"Just hang on, okay? I'm going to call for help. I'll be back in two seconds."

I turned to leave just as he groaned, "No, no ambulances."

I frowned. "Oh, you think you get a say in this?"

He didn't respond.

"I'm going upstairs, and I'm calling nine-one-one."

"No. I...won't go to any hospital," he grumbled.

"So you're a fugitive. I knew it. Where did you escape from? San Quentin? Rikers?"

"No insurance," he muttered.

"Well, that doesn't matter. It's an ER, and you're turning into a block of ice."

"No hospitals."

It dawned on me that maybe he was one of those people who didn't believe in modern medicine. Or, perhaps, he genuinely loathed hospitals. Either way, leaving him here a few minutes longer could mean death.

"Let's get you up. Where are your shoes? Do you have any?" I looked over my shoulder to find perfectly shined black leather boots and a red duffel bag. He also had several books and a reading lamp. Everything was tidy and organized.

I slid his feet into his boots. He didn't even complain despite the bandage on his foot.

"Come on, buddy." I maneuvered him up into a crouch and got him outside. Just past the tent flaps, I noticed an empty bottle of rubbing alcohol. "Is that what you drank? Seriously?"

"Disinfection."

"Oh. Sorry." I shook my head at myself, putting his arm around my shoulders. "You just need to hang on to me. And please, whatever you do, don't complain, insult me or tell me to fuck off. This is happening."

He didn't argue, so we began the ascent. We almost fell a dozen times, but I miraculously managed to keep us upright as the wind howled and whipped through our clothes, numbing my ears.

Once inside the building, I called for Jason, but

he wasn't home, and the other tenant, Mrs. Trudy, took her sleep meds early. A nuke couldn't wake her.

"Just one more flight, buddy. Come on." I urged the man to keep going, using my body for support. Funny, I'd expected him to smell bad, like old onions and trash, but he smelled nice. Like cinnamon.

We got to my front door, and I walked him inside to my couch, where he sprawled out, his large frame barely fitting. I hadn't realized how tall the man was, despite our long haul up the outside steps.

"I'm going to run a warm bath for you. Just wait there." I took off my coat, started running the water, and put the kettle on. By the time I got to him, he was snoring like a lumberjack sawing logs.

"Tent guy?" I gave his shoulder a shake. "You need to warm up. You're freezing." I grabbed my cell from the coffee table to call nine-one-one.

"Please just let me rest…" he mumbled.

"I'm not letting you die on my couch."

"Took a sleeping pill. That's…all. Won't…die." He returned to snoring.

I stood and frowned, testing his hands, forehead and ankle ten times. He was warm. Warm and pink and, well, snoring.

Huh. Strange. Moments earlier he'd been as cold as penguin toes.

I sighed and covered him with my red throw hanging on the sofa arm. "I'm glad you're okay. It would suck to have you die on my big decorating weekend."

But why was he still camping in the alley? Jason said he'd be gone already, and with weather like this, I'd sure be looking for warmer pastures.

I set the thermostat a few degrees higher, flipped off the lights, and went to bed. Yes, I locked my bedroom door and had my cell. Just in case. Like Tent Man said, the world was filled with crazies. Couldn't be too careful. But why did I feel oddly comforted knowing he was in my living room?

CHAPTER SIX

The next morning, I woke to more snow. Not heavy or anything, but just enough to maintain a thick powdery coating on the world outside. I loved how magical it looked, even though it would melt within a few days, leaving behind a mucky brown sludge. By next week, we'd be back in the fifties.

As I stared out my bedroom window, down at the back alley, I could only see a small edge of the red tent, but it was enough to make me feel terrible. There was a person inside, freezing off his chestnuts. He had nothing in this world, including kindness in his heart.

Then my brain kicked on. *Shit. He's in my living room.* How had I forgotten? I'd come to the rescue of a total stranger. Possibly dangerous!

Stop it, Meri. I already knew he wasn't. If the man had wanted to harm me, he probably would've done it already. And he wouldn't have rejected the invitations into my home.

Seriously, I needed to stop assuming anything about him or his life. I knew the world was a complicated place, just like I'd told Jason. Stuff happened. Good stuff, bad stuff, and crushing stuff. Sometimes, life *did* give you more than you could handle.

"Well, you stubborn asshole, I'm not letting it crush you on my account. You'll take my charity and like it." I opened my bedroom door to find the bearded stranger, who smelled like cinnamon, still sleeping on the couch.

"What am I going to do with you?" I muttered. Not like I could send him back outside. But if he refused to go to a shelter, what then?

〰️ 〰️

With breakfast tray in hand, filled with peace offerings—hot coffee, warm pancakes, and fresh orange slices, I hovered over my guest.

"Wakey, wakey. Breakfast cakies," I called out.

He didn't move.

I gave his side a gentle push with my foot. "You okay?"

He cracked open a blue eye. "Who the freak are you?"

Nice greeting. "I'm Meri."

He slowly got to his elbows, his glossy blue eyes sweeping my living room. "Where am I?"

"My place. Don't you remember anything?"

"No." His eyes narrowed on my face. "Oh. It's you."

"What's that supposed to mean?"

He didn't reply. Instead, he pushed his blanket to the floor and attempted to stand, only to stumble back onto my couch.

"You okay?" I asked.

"Yes," he barked. "I'm fine. And you had no right to bring me here against my will."

Against his will? "I saved you." I set the tray down on the coffee table. "So how about a thank you?"

"I don't need saving." He got to his unsteady feet, managing to keep it together this time.

I inhaled sharply, pretending his words didn't sting. As a person who hated conflict and, maybe, who showed overappreciation to the people in my life, it wasn't easy to be slapped for helping a stranger. Then again, I needed to listen to him. Like Shawna'd said, I was addicted to being a people pleaser. Like Kay'd said, I gave with expectations. I had to treat this like a test.

"I hear you. And I'm sorry for helping without asking." I marched to the door. "You're free to leave. I won't stop you or interfere again."

He stared for a long moment, meeting my gaze with a strange, undecipherable expression.

He walked toward the front door, stopping a foot from me. He opened his mouth to speak, only to snap his lips shut.

"What?" I said.

"Sorry for speaking to you so rudely just now," he said flatly. "You're probably not as bad as I thought."

"Is that supposed to be a compliment?"

"Thank you for bringing me into your home. But no matter what happens, you're not to try that again. I can take care of myself." He went out into the hallway and disappeared down the stairs.

"What a jerk."

༻ ༺

I wouldn't talk to Tent Man again for a few weeks, but each night, I'd look out my living room or bedroom window at the visible slice of red next to the dumpster. Why hadn't he moved on yet? And how come my neighbors weren't causing a stink? It was odd on both counts.

On Halloween eve, I'd finally had enough of wondering and decided to talk to the guy.

With a bowl of candy in hand, I made my way down to the alley, prepared to butter him up with gooey, chewy treats before grilling him.

I came out of the gate just in time to spot three teenage boys setting fire to the tent.

"Hey! You little shits! What are you doing?" I yelled.

The three went full-on deer in headlights and then split in the opposite direction.

Oh no. I dumped the candy and ran to the tent, removing my black cat sweater to slap the flames out. "Hey, dude! Your tent is on fire!"

I didn't hear a reply, and fearing he'd maybe taken something to sleep again, I unzipped the front flap, charring my fingertips. "Son of a bitch!"

I looked inside, relieved to see the tent was empty.

I stepped back, watching the fabric melt under the flames.

"What are you doing?" said a deep voice.

I turned to find Tent Man in jeans, a green T-shirt, and boots, staring angrily at me.

"Oh, no," I said. "It wasn't me. Some little fuckers did it."

He rushed over, picked up the tent, and flipped it over. He began stomping out the fire. After a few moments, he'd succeeded, but the damage was done.

"Frosty holidays." He kicked at the mess of smoldering fabric.

I gave him a look.

"I don't swear," he explained.

"Oh." I wasn't sure if his alternative to cussing was cute or just plain strange. "So you're a clean-mouthed homeless man who doesn't believe in seeing doctors."

"I prefer being called a hobo."

I chuckled, thinking he was joking, but his straight-laced expression told me he wasn't. "You really like being called that?" The word conjured up retro cartoon images of a scruffy man with a generous belly, hopping railcars and carrying his worldly possessions in a red handkerchief tied to a stick.

"Yes. Because the world is my home. Ergo, I cannot be home-less. I am home-more."

"Ah. I see. Well, you still need shelter from the elements." I stared at the smoldering mess in front of us. "It's supposed to rain tonight before it drops into the thirties."

"I know," he said.

"I can take you to buy a new tent if you want? The sporting goods place across town has tons of camping stuff, but they won't open until morning. Is there a shelter you'd like to go to?"

"I need to stay here."

"Why?"

"I am waiting for an important package."

Okay. This was just getting weird. "From?"

"From none of your business."

"Fair enough." I nodded, masking my intense curiosity. "Do you know what time the package is coming?"

"I do not, but I cannot miss it," he said.

"Well, you didn't slit my throat last time despite being a serial killer, so I suppose you can crash on my couch again."

He flashed an irritated look at me.

"I'm just trying to help." Though, I really didn't know why.

He looked away, his jaw pulsing beneath a curtain of black bristly whiskers. As I stared, waiting for his reply, I realized he was probably around my age. The beard made him look older, but there was no mistaking the youthful skin under that scowl.

"I'll go first thing after work tomorrow and buy you a new tent, okay?" I added.

"Why are you trying to help me?" he asked accusatorially.

I shrugged. "I guess..." I was about to say something that made me sound like an awesome, selfless giver, but it would be a lie. "It freaks me out, thinking of someone dying under my bedroom window. And honestly, I could use a full night's sleep."

"So you do not actually care about me," he said sternly.

Of course I cared, but I couldn't claim he was a level three yet. Aka a casual acquaintance. "I guess not."

"Good. Because I do not deserve your sympathy or goodwill."

I tilted my head, my mind filling with so, so, sooo many reasons as to why his statement was not a good thing. "What did you do?"

"Nothing."

"Well," I folded my arms, "you must've done something if you think you don't deserve kindness."

"I did nothing."

My mind clicked. So the man was paying penance for something he'd *failed* to do. Perhaps he was like one of those morons you saw on social media who got out their phones and filmed while an innocent granny was being robbed.

He bent down and started picking through the wreckage, collecting his red bag and a partially charred book. I wondered what it was.

"Just so we're clear," he said, "you are not to ask me questions, go through my belongings, or attempt to save me."

"Okay."

"I mean it. I do not need rescue. And certainly not from you."

I nodded. "Understood. No rescuing. No butting in. But I do have one request."

"What?"

"Okay, two, really," I said. "Don't slam the decorations in my apartment, and would you help me pass out candy? I have a big proposal due at work tomorrow, and the people in my building leave out a big bowl of boxed raisins."

"I don't understand. What is wrong with raisins?"

No sane person handed out raisins on Halloween. "Would you like to spend the next two days picking little brown blobs from the mailbox or scraping them from the windshield of your car? Because the kids find really creative ways to give them back."

"That is very mean."

I nodded. "Yep. And it's why I bribe them with full-sized candy bars to leave us alone."

"In my day, naughty children got a lump of coal, not oversized treats."

In his day? Like I'd said, he was probably around my age. "Okay, grandpa. Are you going to help or not? Because I have twenty pounds of diabetes in colorful wrappers that need homes tonight." Plus a ton of work due tomorrow.

"If you count this as working for my keep, then I will help."

I smiled.

"After we pick up this litter." He looked at the candy on the ground. Some of it was probably fine on the inside, but the wrappers were all wet and mucky. No good.

"So you're a clean, non-swearing, prideful hobo. I can respect that."

"And you are a nosy, condescending, overly honest, kind person. I can respect that too."

I was about to argue over his assessment of me, but it didn't really matter what he thought. I would get help with the candy and have a peaceful night's sleep, knowing he wouldn't die under my window.

Seriously though, underneath the excuses, I kept thinking how odd it was. I didn't know the man, yet I sort of liked having him around. Why would a stranger, who could very well end up being a crazy person, inspire a sense of comfort?

CHAPTER SEVEN

"So what is it that you do, exactly?" asked Tent Man as he went through his red bag, looking for something. I noticed how all of his clothes looked clean and were neatly rolled.

"I'm in the insurance business. The name is Meri Winters, by the way. And you?"

"Beau Starling."

"Beau the hobo. Cute." I smiled.

He flashed an annoyed look.

"So, what did you do before this?" I asked.

"You mean before I decided to live like I do now?"

I shrugged. "Sure."

"Nothing worth mentioning."

I frowned and wiggled my lips, hesitating to get nosy but unable to resist. "How long have you been living on the streets?"

"I live in a *tent*, and you said you wouldn't pry."

"Okay. You're right. I'll butt out." But really, my curiosity had dialed up to ten. Every answer he gave convinced me there was a big whopper of a story hiding inside him.

"Thank you." He looked out the window behind the couch, checking for whoever was coming to deliver this mystery package.

"I was about to have some soup for dinner. Would you care to join me?" I asked.

"Thank you, but I'm not hungry. Buying something at the gas station down the street is a requirement to use their facilities. I end up snacking all day."

So he didn't poop in a paper bag. Good to know.

His eyes moved around my living room, taking in the various displays in each corner. "You really like Christmas, don't you?"

I was about to proudly gush over my fanaticism but held back. I was beginning to realize that not everyone shared my sickness: Santa fever.

"I do," I said, leaving it at that.

"Did you make all of these decorations yourself?" He pointed to my appetizer tree and then to the enormous snowman with an ice machine built into his belly. It wasn't a big machine, but it had been a fun project, creating an enormous paper mâché snowman with a little table inside. If you wanted ice, you just lifted his red scarf and reached inside his tummy to the ice container. I'd added blue lights inside, too, for Arctic flair.

"Yeah. It's sort of my thing," I said.

"I like it."

I pushed back a big grin. "It's no big deal."

He turned in place, taking in the lights attached to the ceiling. They weren't plugged in at the moment, but I'd sequenced them to look like runways.

I added, "I need to fix the motor for my miniature Santa and sleigh, but when it's plugged in, they run on a small cable so Santa can travel around the ceiling. It's for a party I throw each year."

We stared at each other for an awkward moment, and I suddenly felt intensely aware of his presence. His tall frame and muscular build took up space like any large man would, but the energy in the room felt different. Warmer maybe?

Maybe it's just me. I'd bet my dancing-elf vibrator that my cheeks were flushed right now.

"Okay, well, I'm going to get cracking on work. There's the candy for passing out." I pointed to two grocery bags by the door and a bright orange bucket. "There's a fold-out chair in the hall closet so you can sit by the mailboxes out front. Just be sure to remind the kids not to revenge-raisin the place."

"Got it." He glanced at the bathroom.

"Oh, uh, make yourself at home. I'll just be in the kitchen on my laptop." I liked working in there for the light. Also, the mint green tile and red appliances gave it a cheery holiday vibe.

"The Y didn't have hot water this morning. Would you mind if I showered?"

My discomfort spiked. It was one thing to let him crash on my couch or use the toilet, but showers were kind of personal. He'd see my lady razor, touch my soap, and judge my shampoo choices—sugar cookies and cream was my favorite at this time of year. I got it from a shop down the street.

"If it's too uncomfortable, I understand," he added.

"No, go right ahead. There are cleaning supplies under the bathroom sink. I mean, in case you feel like bleaching the tub when you're done. Or before you shower. Either-or. Or both. I mean, can't be too careful when it comes to hygiene."

"Thanks. Appreciate it. Also, do you have pen and a paper? I'm going to leave a note in the alley; just in case my delivery comes, they'll know where I am."

"Sure. I'll go get them."

As I spoke, he pulled out a bright red sweater from his bag. It was a gorgeous, handmade piece from the Wild Winterland Clothing Store. They cost over five hundred dollars. Mostly because they used organic, hand-dyed cotton yarn. The quality was so good that some people claimed to have inherited their sweaters from family members, decades old. The question was, how could he afford one?

"You have a Winterland," I said. "Any Rolexes in there, too?"

He gave me a side glance. "No. And the sweater was a gift from my mother."

"Well, she has great taste."

"Had."

My heart twitched with sadness. "I'm sorry. I bet you miss her."

He nodded and disappeared into the bathroom with a handful of stuff.

I exhaled. "What am I doing?" I'd invited this stranger into my home, and clearly I was unable to stop myself from prying. The last thing I needed was to get vested in his life. I had my own things to take care of.

Well, thankfully, he'd be out by morning.

☙ ❧

I didn't see Beau after his shower, but I'd heard him go out the door, so I assumed he'd found the paper and pen I'd left on the coffee table before he went to pay for his keep.

Honestly, I was kind of bummed out having to work on Halloween, because seeing the kids' costumes was the best, almost as fun as watching my nieces and nephews open gifts on Christmas morning. Usually on Christmas Eve, I drove to my parents' house, and I'd stay for a week as friends I grew up with and family would pop in and out for visits. After my big party, which I usually held a few days before Christmas, going to their place to hang out and enjoy some nature, along with seeing people I missed, was a welcome time. I just had to put up with my mom's nagging: *You should go to church more often. Why aren't you married yet? Have you seen my new Brazilian Jesus?*

Around 9:20 p.m., I heard the front door open, followed by heavy footsteps.

"How was the candy giving?" I called out.

Suddenly, a tall man appeared in the kitchen doorway. He had on a forest green ski cap, a black parka, jeans, and perfectly shined black boots.

I screamed. "Who the fuck are you? What do you want? I don't have any money."

He stared, confused.

That was when I noticed him holding my empty candy bucket. He was also wearing Beau's red sweater beneath the parka.

I blinked at the clean-shaved man with crisp-blue eyes and incredible bone structure. He had thick black lashes and slightly arched black brows. "Beau?"

"Does the beard really make me look that different?" He rubbed his smooth, square jaw.

"Errr...yeah." Who knew the man had a face underneath all that hair? He even had lips. Nice plump ones.

Not that I was interested. I liked a man who lived indoors. Then again, I had dated a few men with nice homes but lived like disgusting farm animals.

"I really didn't recognize you. I mean, obviously." I'd just screamed bloody murder.

"I didn't want to scare the little ones," Beau said. "The bushy caveman beard can be intimidating."

Not to me, but I supposed to a tiny child, the wild facial hair might make Beau look a little grizzly bearish. "That was thoughtful."

"And I made sure to clean up the bathroom and sanitize anything I touched, in case you were worried."

Actually, I'd already used the bathroom and had completely forgotten he'd been in there. Not a hair. Not a nasty anything left behind. "Thanks."

"Well, if you don't mind, I think I'll get some sleep." He peeled off his parka and removed his hat.

Wow. He looked like a normal, hot, functional man. No one would guess where I'd met him.

"I left you a pillow and blankets on the couch."

"You still working?" he asked.

"Yeah, just a few more hours. It's just a lot of t-crossing and i-dotting for some big housing development in Texas. Five hundred homes, sewers, gas lines, you know."

"That's interesting."

Nope. It was as boring as hell. I took the job because it paid well, but it didn't feed my soul. Maybe that was why I got into the holidays so much. "Yeah, the builder carries a lot of risk until the project's done and the homes are all sold. Even then, there can be issues if something wasn't built right. It's big business, but big risk, too."

"I don't miss it at all," he muttered.

"Miss what?"

"The stress of work. The late nights. The missing out on life."

Ooh... So he'd once had a busy, stressful life. Lawyer? Doctor? Veterinarian? *Please let it be that last one. Vets are sexy.* "I thought you said you didn't do anything in your pre-hobo life."

"I said I did nothing worth noting. Good night."

What a party pooper. He'd sprinkled breadcrumbs that left me even hungrier for more info and then slammed the door in my face. "Night. Oh, and I'll pick you up a new tent tomorrow after work. The store is just down the street from my office."

"No need. I can handle it on my own."

"You sure? It's no big deal." Also, good winterproof tents were expensive.

"I do not need your help." He disappeared into the living room. "But thank you."

At least this time, he hadn't added the fuck-you tone to his refusal.

I finished my work and then got everything ready for the morning. Coffee, sugar, cereal, bowls, mugs, and silverware. I then realized I had to leave early. What if he wasn't up yet? I'd have to kick him out. Awkward.

I'd just deal with it in the morning.

I tiptoed through the living room, catching the silhouette of my guest's handsome sleeping face. I stared for a moment, thinking about everything my friends had been saying over the last few weeks—the stuff about me being a people pleaser or too self-conscious.

I certainly didn't feel that way around Beau. I was okay if he wasn't pleased or unhappy. I didn't feel the need to impress him or gush about my Christmas addiction. He wasn't even grateful for my hospitality, and I was okay with it.

Honestly, I kind of just enjoyed helping the man. Even if it was only a warm couch for one night. He seemed like the type who was up against something difficult.

The next morning, when I got up for work, Beau was already gone. The blankets were folded neatly, he'd hand-washed a glass he'd used, and he'd left a note:

Meri,

Left you breakfast in the refrigerator. Payment for the night's stay. I also fixed your motor.

   – Beau

I looked up at the ceiling and noticed he'd attached the Santa and sleigh to the cable, too. I then went to the kitchen. Inside the fridge was a stack of chocolate chip pancakes, a bowl of fresh strawberries, and some orange juice.

The weird part was, these weren't my groceries. He'd gone out and bought food. And then prepared everything while I slept. The dishes were done and put away too.

What kind of hobo is this?

CHAPTER EIGHT

I didn't have time to thank Beau before I left for work, but I couldn't stop thinking about him the entire day.

Had he stolen the groceries? Did he panhandle and buy them? Did he get some government check he cashed and used those funds?

That last theory would explain things in terms of him waiting for a package. Maybe he had an acquaintance who cashed his money and gave it to him each month. After all, he looked healthy enough. And apparently, he had a membership to the YMCA. The mystery of my unofficial neighbor was becoming unbearable.

"So? What's your theory?" I asked Shawna toward the end of the day, after I filled her in on all the details.

"My money's on him being a drug mule or working for the mob as some money-laundering go-between."

I nodded, thinking it over. "The package. He was really concerned about being there to receive it."

"Exactly," she said.

"But then why live in an alley?"

"Maybe he's trying to keep a low profile. Who knows?" She tsked. "But, Meri, what the hell were you thinking letting him stay with you? Twice! What if I'm wrong and the package is a head? A big bloody, detached head."

"Gross."

"Can you prove me wrong?" she replied.

"He's not a head trafficker." I rolled my eyes.

"It's not like they just carry them around, Meri. He would have hiding places around the city."

"He doesn't deal noggins. Okay? And I'm being serious. There's something about this guy that's different. And I'm not just talking about the five-hundred-dollar sweater, the mystery package, or the very suspicious breakfast."

"What about it?" she asked.

"He bought groceries this morning and then made breakfast. Pretty delicious, too."

Her eyes went wide. "You ate it?"

"Yeah, why?"

"What if he'd poisoned the food?"

"He's not a psycho killer," I barked, though I wasn't entirely sure about it.

"Well, I agree with you about one thing; he doesn't sound normal."

"Exactly," I said.

"I'm having some friends over tonight. Why don't you bring him so I can check him out?"

"To game night?" Ugh, I hated game night.

Shawna and her friends were way too competitive, which was why I never went. But then again, maybe she could crack this mystery. "I'll see if I can convince him to go. But be nice."

"Never. It's game night." She pointed at me. "But if your man is hiding something big, my friends and I will figure it out. We're all about the puzzles."

She had an excellent point. "See you at eight."

༺ ༻

After work, I found Beau in the alley, assembling a new red tent. And not a cheap one either. It was a well-known brand for extreme conditions, used by climbers.

Where did he get the money? I had to unlock the mystery that was Beau before it drove me crazy.

"So you in?" I asked. "And before you answer, I'm only asking because I can't hurt Shawna's feelings. She's a really, really good friend, but I hate game night. I suck at trivia and drawing and all that crap. Also, they're usually all paired up, and it makes my presence awkward. So what do you say? It'll only be a few hours."

He glanced my way several times, only half listening to me. "I really can't."

"Oh, the package. You have to wait."

"Sadly, no. The window closed."

Huh? "What window?"

"They only deliver on specific days. If at all. Never mind."

"Sorry. Sorry," I groveled. "I know how you feel about people prying."

"Yet you seem to be unable to resist."

True, but did he have to throw it in my face? "She lives in a terrible neighborhood. You wouldn't want me to go alone, would you?"

He stood straight up and planted a hand on his trim waist. "Are you just saying that so I'll go?"

"No?"

He shook his head at me.

"Okay," I huffed. "She lives in a great apartment. Not as charming as mine because it's missing a man in a red tent, but no place is perfect." I smiled big, showing him all of my pearlies.

"You are a very, very strange woman."

"Says the man who's living next to my garbage. So will you come? It's not like you have anything else to do, right?"

"I have a book I'm reading," he said.

"Which one?"

"*A Christmas Carol*. I read it every year."

"A Dickens man." *Hot.* "Okay. Well, I get it. I'll just have to continue my losing streak alone, then." I turned toward the gate.

"Are you implying that I would lose?"

I looked back at him over my shoulder. "Would you?"

"Never."

"Guess we'll never know for sure, will we?"

He shook his head. "You are a terrible manipulator, but I will go."

"You will?" My stomach felt all tingly.

He nodded woefully.

"Yay!" I clapped, jumping up and down. "See you out front in an hour?"

"Yes."

"Thank you, Beau."

"Do not mention it," he said dryly.

I made my way upstairs, feeling giddy until I remembered that I was bringing him to Shawna's under false pretenses. She and her friends were going to try to sniff out the truth about who he was.

I called Shawna, but it went to voicemail. "Hey, it's Meri. Um, I'm bringing Beau with me, but let's just scrap that whole thing about making him the puzzle to solve tonight. Maybe it's better I don't know. See you soon. Bye."

CHAPTER NINE

"You seem nervous," Beau said as we drove toward Shawna's place about fifteen minutes away. She lived near the lake, close to the private marina. "Are you worried about bringing me to meet your friends?"

"Why would I be nervous?"

"Do I need to point out the obvious?" he said.

"You mean that you're now on the hook for ensuring I end my losing streak?"

"It's all right to say what you're really thinking: I'm a hobo." He added, "I chose this life, and I'm not ashamed, so why should you be?"

"I just don't see why we need to talk about something you don't want to discuss. It'll only make me want to pry, and you've made your feelings known about that."

"True."

"I mean, at this point, you've made it clear that you don't want anyone's help; you are tidy and a decent cook. You have money to buy a new tent and groceries, but no job. You have a membership to the Y, and you smell nice. Also, you seem fairly articulate—crunchy and bitter, but articulate—so you're either self-educated, or you completed some form of school. Why would I want to talk about all that? Pfft! How boring."

"Meri, you must believe me when I say that I am not a mystery to be unraveled. I am not starving, destitute, or in need of medical care. I am fully aware of my circumstances and live the way I choose. It's not forever, but for now, this is what I must do."

Must do? Why? "See. There you go again, saying nothing, but really? You're piling on the mystery bricks. It's like you're begging me to grill you."

He sighed with exasperation. "And this is exactly why I don't talk to anyone. They only wish to meddle."

"I'm not meddling. I'm curious. For example, are you happy? I mean, living all alone in a dark, wet, cold alley?"

"That is none of your business," he growled.

We pulled up to Shawna's place, and I parked in a guest spot, turning off the engine.

"I'm smelling deflection, which means you're *not* happy. I'm guessing you *could* change things, but you don't want to. You want to suffer. So tell me why, and I'll leave you alone."

"I don't owe you anything." He leaned in close, locking eyes with me. I noticed how his cheekbones curved down toward his upper lip, accentuating their fullness somehow. He really was handsome.

And looking a little pissed off. It was time to back off. "You owe me a win." I hopped out of my red truck. "Coming?"

He grumbled something under his breath and got out. Silently, we made our way to Shawna's townhouse. Once we got to the front door, I rang the bell and turned towards him.

"I'm sorry," I said. "I know I promised not to butt into your life. I'll stop. But if we lose tonight, I'm burning your new tent."

He shook his head at me. "I don't lose."

Strange thing to say for a man in his position, whom some might call a loser. But I was beginning to see he was anything but that. He was tough and stubborn. He was articulate and self-reliant.

So who was Beau Starling?

CHAPTER TEN

True to his word, Beau helped me crush the other ten people here at Shawna's tonight, and luckily, she had gotten my message. Her friends knew nothing about Beau ahead of time, but it hadn't prevented them from being curious or asking questions. Of course, Beau kept things vague, and I wasn't the only one consumed with intrigue.

As it started getting late, Shawna's sister, Egypt, cornered me in the all-white, immaculate kitchen (Shawna didn't cook).

"How do you two know each other?" she asked.

"Neighbors."

"Acquaintances? Just friends?"

What was with the twenty questions? "Yes to both," I replied, filling my glass with water.

"Is he single?"

I felt my hackles rise. Yes, I'd just told her that he and I were friends, which was almost true, but it still felt like she was stomping through my garden, stepping on my flowers.

"Egypt, Beau is a pretty private guy, and I really don't know that much about him, but I seriously doubt he's open to a hookup if that's what you're after."

"Hookup?" She jerked her head of short dark curls to the side. "I'm too old for that shit, and he is one fine man. Just trying to get a feel for his situation is all." She poured herself a fresh glass of white wine from the fridge. "I mean, are we talking Manhattan or Louisianna? Burbs or farmland?"

"I'm not sure I understand—"

"Meri, men are like topographical maps. They have highs spots, low spots, and gradations. If you can figure out what their map looks like—are they mountains with peaks, swamp, or pastures?—then you know what you're getting. You'll know if you can thrive in their environment or not. 'Cause one thing I've learned about men is that they don't change. What you get is what you get. Take it or leave it."

I didn't agree at all. Men could change, just like anyone else. "I've never heard that particular analogy before. But I don't know what sort of terrain Beau is, and I think you should leave him alone."

"Why? You just said you're not dating him," she said.

"Correct."

"Do you wanna date him?" she asked.

"No," I replied firmly. I mean, who would want to date a guy with such a bizarre life?

"Then step aside, Christmas kitten, and let me

survey. M'kay?"

"Kitten?" I arched a brow.

"We all know you live for the soft, fluffy crap served during the holidays."

"I like Christmas. So how's that soft or fluffy?"

"Have you ever gone on an American Horrorday vacation? Imagine being in the woods in a rundown cabin, the night air filled with screams as campers are chased by bloody elves. It's like Freddy meets the North Pole. Nonstop cosplay gore. Plus all the holiday horror movies you can stomach. I go every year with a big group."

"Sounds…interesting." I didn't know what else to say. As far as I was concerned, she could keep her weird murder-Christmas. *Just hands off Beau.* "Guess I am a Christmas kitten after all. Meow."

"And I'm a surveyor of men." She laughed and went out to the living room.

As the evening wore on, I sat with Shawna on her zebra print couch, across from her friend Roy, who was a high school teacher by day and sculptor by night. He was also a sniffling moron whose passion was talking about anything meaningless. *"I think rosé wines are for people who cannot commit to red or white. I read a study done in Italy, and they found that rosé drinkers are ten times more likely to divorce."*

Ohmygod. Shut up! That was what I'd wanted to say when Shawna first introduced us a few years ago, hoping we might click. We had not. He wasn't even level-four friend material—aka "acquaintances through a friend"—in my book. If I ever spotted him in a store, I would pretend I didn't see him.

"I love your new zebra couch, Shawna," Roy said, sitting in the black velveteen armchair. "Did I tell you that I went to the zoo recently? I think it's a waste that they don't sell the elephant dung. Think of all the money they could make off that prime fertilizer. I read that elephant dung can make your fruit trees grow ten times bigger."

Someone please shove toothpicks in my ears. I looked over at Beau and Egypt sitting across the room at the dining room table with the other guests. She'd moved one inch closer to him, and now she had her daggers on his arm. To his other side was one of Shawna's good friends, Mona, giggling and batting her eyelashes.

I can't believe this. They're all over him! Rage began bubbling inside. It wasn't that I owned him or anything, but he'd come with me. He wasn't here for them.

"Meri, why are you looking like an angry ripe tomato?" Shawna whispered.

"Can I speak to you alone in the kitchen?" I said to her in a low voice.

Roy gave me a hard look. "Secrecy causes liver damage. Did you know that a study—"

"If you say one more word, Roy," I growled, "I'll study your liver over a cheap Chianti." I dragged Shawna to the kitchen.

"What's up?" she asked.

"I thought you called off the Beau inquisition."

"I didn't say a word to anyone."

"Then why's your sister and friend all over him?" I seethed.

"Maybe because he's hot?"

"No, he isn't," I protested.

"You're telling me that the tall guy out there with sultry bedroom eyes and a jaw like a nutcracker isn't hot?"

I lowered my voice. "He lives in my alley next to a dumpster."

"That doesn't make him unfuckable."

My jaw dropped. "You're telling me you'd let Egypt, your little sister, take some hobo to bed?"

"She's a grown-ass woman. Besides, why are you acting all jealous? Do you want him, Meri?"

"No."

She grinned, a teasing look in her eyes. "Then why'd you call and say to leave him alone? You're trying to protect him."

"I'm not," I grumbled.

"Then just let him be. Let her be. She can make up her own mind about him." She looked out the kitchen doorway at Beau, her face glowing.

"Ohmygod. You like him, too, don't you?" I said.

"Maybe? I mean, look at the man. And he just whipped everyone's asses at trivia, charades, and hangman. Brains and looks. He can pitch his tent at my place anytime." She chuckled.

That was it.

I marched over to Beau, who still sat happily at the table, chatting away with his admirers. "Time to go."

"So soon?" Egypt said.

"Yeah. I have...stuff to do tomorrow. Christmas-kitten stuff. You know," I said bitterly.

Beau looked at me. "Are you okay?"

No, I was angry. Everyone was hitting on my hobo. "Yep. All good. Let's go."

"You can stay if you want," said Mona. "I can give you a lift home." She slid her arm over his bulging bicep.

In that moment, I didn't know what came over me, but it wasn't something good. "The guy lives in a tent, okay? His home is my apartment's dumpster. He's not my friend or neighbor. He's a bum. A homeless bum. I'm sorry for bringing him here, but it seemed like the nice thing to do."

The room fell silent, and instead of pushing away from Beau, Mona and Egypt snarled at me.

"You're a mean bitch," said Mona.

"Yeah. Where do you get off talking about someone like that?" said Egypt.

"Meri, seriously?" said Shawna. "What's the matter with you? Everyone is welcome in my home regardless of their financial circumstances."

"I told you she was rude," added Roy. "It's the way she wears her scarf. The knot gives it away every time."

My innards sank to the floor along with my gaze. I knew they were right. Why had I said that? It wasn't like me to snub someone like I'd just done, proof being that I'd invited the guy into my home.

"I-I am so sorry I said that, Beau. I don't know what's wrong with me."

"Neither do I," he said.

I inhaled slowly, the weight of shame urging me out the door to find a hiding place. "I'll go now, but I am sorry. Clearly you're more than your circumstances." With that pathetic apology, I left.

CHAPTER ELEVEN

Saturday morning, Beau wasn't in his tent. I immediately texted Shawna, asking where I might find him, but she was either ignoring me or was still asleep.

Dammit. I texted Kay to let her know I'd be missing spin class again and to go without me.

> **Kay:** *You'd better not be out shopping, girl. Angry face emoji.*

I was too embarrassed to tell her the truth. I'd behaved like a Krampus to a man who hadn't deserved it. I'd called him a bum! *Oh God...*

> **Me:** *I wish, but no. I have some work to catch up on. Sad face emoji.*

I went back upstairs, deciding to write a note to Beau. Then I thought that a note wouldn't do, so then I baked some pumpkin spice muffins with cream cheese frosting.

I put them in a plastic container and placed a red bow on top. I could only pray he'd forgive me for last night, but why had I done it? That had been a full-blown, she-devil meltdown, kind of like a mamma bear, only I wasn't his mamma. I'd acted like a jealous girlfriend.

Do I like him? But he wasn't my type. I mean, apart from being hot. And mysterious. And sort of kind in that none kiss-assy way that I liked. But the man had no job or home, and he came with some very sharp edges.

Yeah, I wonder why, Meri, I scolded myself. It was no wonder he didn't want help from anyone. He was probably tired of all the judging when he was perfectly content with his way of life. He'd said so himself.

Then here I came, meddling, talking down to him in front of my friends, and being an all-around shithead. Maybe Kay was right about me not being a genuine giver. Not from the heart. Not in a good-spirited way. If I wanted to change that, I had to begin by being kinder and to apologize from the heart.

I rewrote my note, simply asking to talk. I then grabbed the muffins and headed downstairs, but when I got to the alley, the tent was gone.

Oh no. Where did he go? I couldn't leave things between us like this.

I was about to go back up and ask if Jason knew where Beau might've gone when a white delivery truck pulled up. The man inside wore a red jumpsuit and matching baseball cap.

He looked up at the building and checked his

phone. He then rolled down the window. "Is this 1225 Peppermint Street?"

"Yes, but the front door is one street over."

"Have you seen a man with a red tent around here?"

Was this the delivery Beau had been waiting for? "Yes, he's been sort of staying with me." I was about to add that he'd also been camping out here and had taken off to God only knew where, but the man cut me off.

"Well, in that case," the man handed me a small red box with a white bow on top, "can you see that he gets this?"

"Sure." I took the box, praying I could track Beau down.

The man dipped his head and then sped off down the alley. The back of the truck read Starling Toys. There was a cartoon of a little reindeer with a red nose, too.

So weird. I went back inside and knocked on Jason's door. He answered in his boxers, scratching his bed head. "What's the matter?" he grumbled.

"Have you seen Beau?"

"Beau?"

"Yeah, the guy living in the alley."

"No. Why?" he asked.

"Someone just gave me a package for him, but I'm not sure where he's gone," I explained.

"Haven't seen the guy in weeks."

I frowned. "Weeks?"

"Yeah, since that first time you complained. I made sure he'd be gone before the weekend, and he took off that day."

What? "No. He definitely stuck around."

Jason gave me a confused look. "You sure about that? Because I'm back there all the time, grabbing tools and stuff from my garage."

"Jason, he has a bright red tent. How could you not see him?" I argued.

He shrugged, and I could tell he was wondering if I'd lost it.

"I'm telling you," I said. "He didn't leave. Not until this morning."

"I don't know what to say, Meri. I haven't seen anyone."

What the hell? Was he playing a trick on me? How could he not notice Beau for four weeks?

Suddenly, Mrs. Trudy came out of her apartment next door to Jason's, her silver hair up in a bun. She wore five layers of sweaters over her house dress.

"Hey, Mrs. Trudy," said Jason, "have you seen a man hanging around in the alley lately?"

"No. But someone hasn't been separating their recycling again." She gave me a harsh look.

She went through my trash? "I ran out of space in my recycle container. It was just one yogurt cup."

She shook her head. "You lazy people are destroying the planet."

Jeez. It was just one time. "Are you sure you

haven't seen anyone living by the dumpster, Mrs. Trudy? Red tent? Tall?" *Sexy jawline?*

"No. I would've told Jason. We can't have vagabonds living anywhere they like, all willy-nilly. Why do you think I give ten percent to the church?"

Mrs. Trudy? Give ten percent? She was so cheap that I once caught her putting her dirty clothes in with someone else's at the laundromat down the street. Gross. Also, she frequently picked the lock on my mailbox and stole my coupons. Meanwhile, she drove a Benz. And not one of those old diesel-guzzling monsters either.

"Okay, well, if you see the guy, will you let me know?" I said. "I have a package for him."

"I'll call the police is what I'll do," said Mrs. Trudy.

I sighed with exasperation and went upstairs. It made no sense how the other tenants hadn't noticed Beau in over a month. Were they that self-absorbed and blind to the homeless?

Desperate to find Beau, I called Shawna again, but it went to voicemail.

With no other options, I grabbed my purse and keys and headed out.

☙ ❧

I ended up driving around the city, hitting the shelters, parks, and bus station, but there was no sign of Beau. By the time I got home, it was pouring rain outside and freezing cold. The thought of him wandering around, trying to get dry and warm, made my heart ache.

Of course, that was foolish of me. Beau wasn't stupid or without resources. He knew how to take care of himself, even if it was under uncomfortable circumstances.

So where would a man like him go?

I made some hot tea, my mind spinning. I wanted to make things right, but how? I had to start by finding him and delivering this package.

The package... I eyed the red box on my coffee table. What was inside? It had to be something important. *Maybe it'll give me a clue to where he went.*

No, you're just being nosy. "I'm not opening you. Do you hear me, red box? Not happening."

But as the seconds ticked by, I knew I was about to do something terribly wrong.

I reached for the box, untied the ribbon, and looked inside. I don't know what I was expecting, but not this. *A letter.*

I unfolded the thick parchment:

Beau,

I received your last petition, and while you say you've truly repented for your past, I see that you still haven't changed.

I urge you to stop playing games because time is almost up.

If you ever want to see her again, you know what you must do.
   — Dad

My hands began shaking. "See her again?" Was his own father holding someone Beau loved as a hostage? His wife? His daughter? Who? And how could his own father do this to him? What had Beau done?

It doesn't matter. Because it was clear to me that Beau's dad was punishing him for something. Maybe it was for something terrible, but this was no way to treat your child.

When I'd been caught cheating on a test in high school, my dad didn't yell or punish me. He told me how much he loved me and then cried like a little kid. He'd said that my failures were his and that he hadn't done his job properly. Otherwise, why would I have done something so stupid?

Now, you might say to yourself, *"What a kind, sensitive parent,"* but no. My dad was a guilt pirate. He said all that stuff because he understood that parental guilt was the best weapon in his fatherly arsenal. Because there was nothing more terrifying than seeing your father cry. Needless to say, I never cheated again.

In any case, it appeared that this entire situation was about punishing Beau with massive guilt. *That poor woman.* I could only hope they weren't torturing her while Beau attempted to appease his evil dad.

I had to help him. But first, I had to find him.

"Beau." I shook my head with a sigh. "Where did you go?"

CHAPTER TWELVE

Four weeks went by, and there'd been no sign of Beau or his tent. I put ads in the classifieds, posted flyers around the city, and stuck a laminated letter on my garage door by the dumpster, in case Beau came by.

Beau, package came for you. Keeping it safe.

— Meri

Shawna wasn't talking to me much anymore—just a few polite words here and there at work—but she'd mentioned that she didn't know where Beau had gone after the party. Also, she said she didn't want to be friends anymore because I was a mean person.

I guessed I wasn't the saint everyone believed, and the real me, the one with a jealous side, wasn't to their liking. So which was it? Was I too nice, too much of a people pleaser? Or was I too imperfect? Too flawed?

I wasn't really sure, but I knew one thing: I was me, a living, breathing work in progress, and I always had been. I'd never claimed to be perfect, so why wasn't I good enough all of a sudden?

I was beginning to think the problem wasn't me at all. Maybe my friends were changing. Or maybe I was. Both?

Either way, I'd always accepted and loved them for who they were. For example, Kay was caught up in her looks, but that was okay. I understood why, and she had a heart of gold. Shawna was a stone-cold teardown artist who loved using humor to highlight the truth of things. I found it refreshing and hilarious because I knew there was nothing but love inside her heart. If I went down the list of every single cherished person in my life, they all had at least one outrageous flaw or quirk, but I loved them anyway.

So…so…screw them. I'm not going apologize anymore for who I am. Not like they were running around asking for grace over their icky sides.

That didn't mean I wasn't sorry for my screwup at game night. I felt mortified by my behavior, and I'd apologized. So why wasn't I allowed to make a mistake? Everyone else in the world was given room to grow and learn.

As for Beau, I could only assume he'd moved on to a new city or country. It scrambled my mind how a stranger could walk into my life like that and flip everything on its head. Suddenly, I just didn't care about my party. I hadn't even sent out invitations or started shopping for gifts. Friendsgiving was tonight, and I couldn't care less.

"Who am I?" Lying in bed, piles of dirty bowls and mugs on my nightstand, my cell rang. It was Kay.

"Hello?" I grumbled.

"Are you sick? Is that why you stopped going to the gym and haven't been answering my messages?"

"What do you want?" I asked.

"Meri, what's going on with you?"

I hadn't told her about game night. Too horrifying. "Figuring things out. That's all."

"Are you pouting again about not spending yourself into the poorhouse for Christmas? I never made you sign up for that cruise. You wanted to go."

"I know. But don't worry, Christmas is dead to me now."

"What? What happened?"

"Nothing." I sighed. "I need to get some sleep. Have a good Friendsgiving tonight."

"You're not coming?" she asked.

"No."

"But how can I have Friendsgiving without my best friend?"

"The same way you can tell me I'm not welcome if I don't bring a plus one." *I'm minus one. Minus a heart and the will to shop or brush my freaky hair.*

"Pfft! You know that's not really mandatory. Meri, what's going on with you? Is it because you're turning the big three-oh soon? Talk to me."

My birthday was just around the corner, but that wasn't it.

I started to tear up. "It's all going to shit, Kay." I went on, explaining what had happened on game night and how I was beginning to see that I was an imperfect person in more ways than one or fifty. "But what kills me isn't that my friends won't accept me for who I am or where I am in life at my age, it's that I hurt someone who deserved my genuine acceptance. I showed my ugliest side at the worst possible moment. I acted selfishly."

"So your claws came out," she concluded.

"Yes."

"Well, about time, Meri! I mean, come on. You never say a mean word to anyone even when they deserve it. And now you acted a little immature over a guy. So what?"

"You're not going to disown me now, too?"

"Hell no. But you do need to start being honest with me. Did you ever really want to go on that cruise?"

"No. Not really." If I could choose, I'd do the whole Arctic travel thing.

"So why did you'd keep saying you wanted to go?" she asked.

"Because I love you. And I *did* want to go. I still do."

"But for me," she deducted.

"Yes."

"And the fact I've been pressuring you to save money for a trip you're not entirely passionate about probably made you feel miserable."

"No." I shook my head, even though she couldn't see me. "Okay, maybe at first. But then I started to realize you were right. I was spending money, going all out for this one party each year, when there's more to life." I sighed. "It was a good wake-up call."

"Maybe so, but I'm sorry for saying you wouldn't be my best friend if you didn't go on that trip."

"I forgive you." I sniffled.

"Good. Because I think Lick wants to go. He actually brought it up on his own, so…"

"That's great." *Lick. Lick wants to lick life in the balls.*

"You're making fun of his name in your head right now, aren't you?" she scolded.

"Maybe."

She chuckled. "I love you, Meri. You are so…so…"

"Fucked up?"

"Wonderfully weird. And loyal. So now you need to get your ass over here for turkey."

"Kay, I really don't feel like—"

"Uh, sorry," she cut me off, "but this is not a cruise. This is a dinner that I'm cooking. All you have to do is show up, open your piehole, and shove food inside."

"I don't have a date."

"No problem. I picked up a few extra strays today. We have a full house of eighteen."

I groaned. "Fine. I'll be there."

"Good. Could you bring a pie? Anything, even frozen. I burned mine while we were talking."

She hung up before I could protest. She knew I didn't do frozen baked goods, but there wasn't time to make anything from scratch.

Turning over new leaves left and right, Meri. It's a new day.

CHAPTER THIRTEEN

With frozen pumpkin pie in hand, I entered Kay's place wearing green sweats and a "Gobble Gobble" turkey T-shirt. The turkey was displaying its butthole. Felt appropriate for my mood, which was also reflected in the sloppy, wild frizz ball on top of my head and zero makeup. I just didn't have the holiday Jedi skills to battle the death star of self-ridicule spinning in my chest. But on the bright side, today I'd been reminded of why Kay had been my best friend since middle school, when I became the village ho without the ho-ing. *Stupid Kevin.*

"Hey all," I said, greeting the room of happy, half-lit people. There was Kay's coworker, Kay's sister and brother in-law, and a friend from college and her husband. The rest were an assortment of people I didn't know or whom we'd both met over the years. Shared friends.

The nice thing about Kay's place was that she worked in real estate and generally scored pretty nice deals. This loft apartment had huge windows, views of the glittering skyline, and tons of room. With the modern furniture and concrete floor, it was a little sterile for my taste, but there was no beating her chef's kitchen and twenty-person feasting table fit for any king and queen.

"Hey, is that for me? Thanks." Kay came rushing from the kitchen, taking my pie. "There's someone you need to meet." I followed her to the massive kitchen, finding a tall man, with caramel skin and hazel eyes, whipping mashed potatoes. He wore a big turkey hat and an apron that read, *"Man gravy is the best gravy."*

He took one look at my shirt and laughed. "Good one."

"Back at you, gravy man." For some reason, I'd been expecting him to be the serious type, chanting Buddhist meditations in the corner. This one had a sense of humor.

"Lick, this is Meri. Meri, Lick," said Kay.

I cracked up. "Lick…"

"Oh, stop it," said Kay.

"Sorry." I made a polite wave to Lick. "So is your gravy considered vegan? Kay keeps threatening to quit meat."

He stopped stirring and then laughed.

"See," I said to Kay, "he gets me."

She rolled her eyes.

"Can I help with anything?" I asked. "Or should I leave the kitchen so he can lick your pie before it goes in the oven?"

Kay slapped my arm. Lick chuckled.

"What? I heard that was your superpower," I

said to him.

Kay's eyes went wide, but Lick kept chuckling and stirring. "Yes, ma'am."

"Too much?" I asked Kay.

"A bit." She squeezed her thumb and index finger together. "Oh, crap. I almost forgot to tell you. You won't believe who I ran into…" Her voice faded as I heard the front door, followed by the group in the living room greeting someone.

"They're here," Kay said with a big smile.

"Who?" I asked. "Does Lick have a sister named Tequila? A salty uncle perhaps?"

"You're so lame. I was out shopping today and bumped into Shawna."

A lump of coal formed in my stomach. "My Shawna?"

"Yeah. And I invited her."

They knew each other after attending my annual Christmas parties.

"Why did you invite her? She totally hates me now," I said.

"No," Kay hissed, "she doesn't. You two just need to talk. That's all."

I looked away. "This is the last thing I needed right now." More confrontation.

"Would you trust me for once?" She began shoving me out toward the living room.

I immediately spotted Shawna wearing big orange overalls with slices of pie printed all over them.

Shawna waved, which was a surprise.

I walked over to greet her. "Hey. Happy Thanksgiving. Didn't know you'd be here," I said cheerfully.

"I ran into Kay at the store." She gave me a hug.

"It's great you came," I said, trying to do my best not to let this get weird.

"I don't know about that." She chuckled. "I caught Kay buying gravy in a jar."

Trust me. That's better than the alternative. "What she lacks in the culinary arts, she makes up for in people skills," I said.

"Unlike me?" Shawna said.

"I didn't say that."

"You should." Shawna took my hand. "I'm really sorry about the way I've been acting. I can't believe what a rude bitch I've been."

I shrugged. "I deserved it."

"No. You didn't. I should've thought about all the years you've been such a solid friend. You have the biggest heart in the world, and you never ask for anything except to show up to your place once a year and sing and eat. Maybe puke a little, too, to make room for dessert. But you're a good person, and I'm sorry for treating you like garbage."

I drew a breath. It felt good to hear. "Apology accepted. That is if you'll forgive how I acted at game night."

"Not your best moment, but it wasn't me you hurt. It was your friend Beau."

"I know. And I tried to apologize again, but he

disappeared. Now I'll have to spend the rest of eternity feeling like a turd."

Her eyes darted over my shoulder. "Good thing I bumped into him on the way here and brought him along. Kay insisted when I called ahead to make sure she had room for one more."

He was here? Now?

I turned my head. Standing behind me was a tall, hot drink of holiday goodness. His sweater was red and white striped with a pumpkin in the middle.

His blue eyes locked on my face.

"Beau?" I threw my arms around his neck. "Thank God."

He slowly pried me off.

"I've been looking everywhere for you," I said. "I'm so, so sorry about what I said."

"I know."

"You're not angry?" I asked.

"No."

"Then why did you leave like that?"

"It was time to go," he said.

I was about to ask where he'd run off to, but I suddenly remembered his package. "Some guy stopped by the day you disappeared. He left a package."

His smile melted away into smashed lips and furrowed brows. "Where is it?"

"At my place."

"Let's go." He stepped around me, heading for

the door.

I stayed put. "Kay really worked hard. I can't—"

"I need that package." His hand was on the doorknob. "Let's go."

Wow. His reaction was unexpectedly harsh. "There was just a note inside."

"You opened it?" He came over and glared down at me.

Uh-oh. I had to come clean, but he wasn't going to be happy. "I was hoping it would tell me where you—"

"What did it say?"

"Sorry?" I said.

"I know you read it."

Dammit. How does he know? I stalled for a second and then flubbered out a breath. "It said you weren't forgiven, and that if you ever wanted to see *her* again, you needed to step up because the clock was ticking. Who is she, Beau?"

His handsome face turned into a blank sheet. Maybe he was stunned. Or hurt? I couldn't tell.

"Beau, I am sorry for reading the letter, but you can trust me if you need hel—"

He turned and walked right out the front door.

"Beau! Wait!" I didn't want him to disappear again.

I glanced over my shoulder toward the kitchen. *I can't ditch this dinner, but...*

I rushed to find Kay. "Hey, um, I'll be right back, okay. Beau just left."

"Already? What happened?"

"I'm not sure, but don't start eating without me." I rushed outside to go find Beau.

※ ※

I finally caught up to Beau and his long legs one block down from Kay's building. He looked like a man who needed to be left alone, stomping his way down the sidewalk in the dark, but I had to find out what was happening.

I came up behind him. "Where are you going?"

He kept walking as cars zoomed by, hitting me in the face with their headlights. "Go back to your party, Meri."

"It's freezing out here. Let's go inside and talk."

"Why? What will talking accomplish?" He continued marching along.

"I don't know. Maybe it'll make you feel better. I mean, if my dad were holding someone hostage to punish me, I'd have a lot to say about it."

He finally stopped and turned to face me. "Hostage? What are you talking about?"

I stopped, too. "His letter said if you wanted to see *her* again, you'd have to try harder. Who is she?" I asked.

He shook his head, letting out a long, exasperated sigh. "She is not a person. *She* is his factory."

"Oh. Well, that's good news, but why won't he let you see it?"

"It's a long story, Meri."

"Normally I'd say I've got time to listen, but there's a bunch of hungry people waiting for us to go back to the party, so give me the short version."

"I'm not going back, and my problems are none of your concern."

What a stubborn ass. "Fine, then consider it your parting gift. Solve the mystery that's been swimming in my head for weeks. Put me out of my misery. Who are you? What's going on?"

I expected him to tell me to pound sand, but instead he let out another breath. "The short version is that I am not a good man, Meri. I have done things that cannot be undone. And though I have tried to make amends, I'm realizing it will never be enough to be forgiven. Not by me or him."

"You mean your dad."

"Yes." He ran a hand through his thick dark hair.

"What did you do?" I asked.

"I killed three people."

My stomach flipped. I hadn't been expecting that. "You mean, like, with a gun?"

"No." He sounded offended.

"Did you run them over with your car?" I asked.

"Meri."

"Sorry." I held up a palm.

"I-I was left in charge of the factory for the week, and it caught fire. We lost three workers, and dozens more were injured."

A wave of relief washed over me. Not that I was dancing on these people's graves, because, yikes. Who would do that? But a fire was a far cry from murder.

"So it was an accident," I concluded.

"One that could have been prevented if I had stayed to watch over things. But I did not. I flew to New York and partied with friends for three days. When I got back, it was to a collapsing roof and body bags."

How awful. "But fires happen, Beau."

"Yes. And if I'd been there, I would have ensured everyone was alerted the moment there was an issue. I would've evacuated the building in an orderly fashion instead of the workers scrambling to put out the flames."

Those were a lot of "would haves." It sounded like he was taking the blame for a series of unfortunate events. "Beau, you couldn't have known all that would happen."

"Oh, but I did. My father warned me a dozen times that managing the factory is not about meeting production numbers. It's about making sure our workers make it home safely."

"What kind of things did you make?" I asked.

"Toys."

"Like dolls, trains, and action figures?" The way he'd made it sound, they were making bombs or something.

"Yes. Starling Toys."

The same name on that delivery truck. "I wasn't aware that toy production was such a risky business."

"Wood, paper, plastic, paint—all highly flammable in a factory setting. We make five hundred different items, and there are machines with gears, grinders, paint hoses, and everything else you can imagine. It's easy to just look away for one moment and get a hand caught. Or for a worker who's not paying attention to mishandle a bin of wood shavings. We take safety seriously, but things happen. And I wasn't there to put the fire out when it did."

I touched his arm. "I'm so sorry, but you made a mistake. You didn't hurt anyone on purpose."

"Tell that to their children and spouses. I deserve what I've gotten."

"So that's what this whole thing is about? The tent, the living in the freezing cold, the—"

"I gave up my position and quit the business. It wouldn't bring back their loved ones, but I couldn't look the workers or my father in the eyes again. I'd had everything handed to me in life—even my own house—but I failed to care about what truly mattered: the workers I was watching over, who depended on me. So I left with nothing but the clothes on my back."

He left behind all responsibility, too. "Like a vow of poverty?"

"Something like that. I hitched rides on trains,

cargo ships, whatever. I go where I can find odd jobs to pay for food and necessities. I've learned to survive without depending on anyone."

Good for him, but that sounded extremely lonely, not to mention difficult. "But torturing yourself isn't going to bring anyone back. You have to forgive yourself and move on."

"I have. I have traveled the world and seen suffering, misery, and starvation. I have watched people die of drug overdoses, get shot, stabbed, blown up, run over, starve, drown—"

"Okay. Death. Lots of death. Got it." *Jeez. Dark much?*

"And what I learned is that despite all that, there is still happiness in the world, but it needs more. That is when I finally understood that the business my father is in was never about pride or status. He believes in bringing happiness to the world, especially children. When I finally asked to come back and help him in whatever capacity he chose—warehouse, line worker, whatever—he refused. He said that I would never step foot inside the factory again until I'd changed."

So that was what he meant in his letter. "But why is time almost out?" I asked.

"He's getting ready to retire," Beau said.

"And?"

"He plans to shut down the factory. Permanently."

That was odd. "Didn't he just rebuild it? I

mean, after the fire?"

"That was ten years ago."

My jaw dropped. "How long have you been living on the road?"

"Ten years."

Jesus. "And how long have you been trying to go back?"

"Eight."

Eight years? He'd been asking for forgiveness for eight freaking years. "What does your dad want from you? What's his definition of change?"

Beau scrubbed his face with his hands. "It doesn't matter now. It's over. I have to accept that he was probably never going to allow me to return. Maybe this was his way of teaching me a lesson."

"A lesson in what?" *Turning your back on your children when they royally fuck up?*

"Disappointment."

"Oh, Beau." I squeezed his arm again.

"Do not feel sorry for me. I deserve this. And it is time for me to move on—accept that some things cannot be undone no matter how much you wish it."

I smiled softly, hoping he might feel better knowing that there was at least one person who didn't agree that all was lost.

"Well," I said in a cheery voice, "then consider tonight the beginning of a fresh start. You'll meet some very nice people and enjoy the night of friendship. Also, gluttony. Tonight your life of deprivation ends."

"I should just get going." He glanced in the direction he'd been walking.

"To where, Beau? To your tent?"

"There's a bus leaving for the Mexican border in an hour."

A flutter of panic began dancing in my stomach. I didn't want him to go. "Mexico sounds good. Probably a lot warmer than here, but...if it's really over, then why keep torturing yourself? Stay. Start a new life."

He looked down at his feet. "I'm not sure I can."

"You haven't even tried." I had to convince him to stay. He'd started to occupy a space in my head, and I liked it. I liked him. "It's only one dinner, and Kay's stuffing is fairly edible. The turkey isn't bone dry. After that, you can decide what comes next. There'll always be more busses to Mexico."

"I would...enjoy that," he said and then gazed down, the streetlamp catching the subtle blues of his eyes. "Why are you so kind to me?"

I smiled timidly, my cheeks warming. "Don't you know? I'm really into Christmas, and you remind me of a big box under the tree."

"I'm hardly a gift."

"But you are a mystery, waiting to be unwrapped." I shrugged. "What can I say? It's my thing."

"Are you saying that *I'm* your thing?"

My heart picked up the pace. "You'll have to stick around long enough to find out." I took his hand and squeezed it.

"Stick around." He bobbed his head, mulling over the idea.

"One dinner at a time, Beau. One breakfast, lunch, and dinner at a time."

"You must be hungry for that not bone-dry turkey."

I *was* hungry. But not for food. "I'm famished."

CHAPTER FOURTEEN

"That was more enjoyable than I thought," said Beau as we drove toward my place after dinner.

"Kay does make it fun. I especially like playing Who's the Turkey?" During dinner, everyone was assigned a card with a Thanksgiving dish written on it—green beans, gravy, sweet potatoes, etc.—and we all took turns guessing who got the turkey card. If you guessed wrong, you had to drink or take a punishment from the person you incorrectly called out, like singing a song, tap dancing for twenty seconds, or eating those nasty canned yams. If you guessed the turkey correctly, you got to hand out drinks or punishments to the entire group. If you happened to have the turkey card, then you pretended you didn't and played along until you were directly called out. I don't think we'd ever made it past three rounds until tonight.

"How did you guess the turkey five times in a row?" I asked.

"I can tell when people are lying or hiding something. It's a gift."

"So you have a built-in BS meter?" I stopped at

a light.

"Something like that."

"So tell me, what am I hiding?" I asked.

"You really want to know?"

"Hmmm...maybe not. I've had a lot of frank feedback from my friends lately. And let's just say I'm working through some things now."

"Such as?" he asked.

"Apparently, I am a people pleaser, I have an unhealthy obsession with Christmas, and I spend too much on other people. I'm also overly self-conscious but not self-aware enough—whatever that means." I turned my head and waited for his reaction.

He didn't really have one.

The light turned green, and we continued on.

After a few minutes, his lack of response started making me uneasy. Finally, when we pulled up to my building, I had to ask. "Are you just going to leave me hanging?" I said as I shut off the engine.

He looked over, his face unreadable.

"What?" I snapped.

"I think I'm drunk."

I started to laugh. "But you hardly drank anything."

"Shawna made me do shots with her while you were in the kitchen helping put the food away."

Shawna had liquored him up. "Did she hit on you?"

"Absolutely."

I felt my jealousy rear its ugly head again, so I stomped on it. "Well, she's very pretty and a good person. I can't blame you for being interested." I looked away, hiding my disappointment. *Why even care, Meri? It's not like this—us—was ever going anywhere.*

"Yes, she is very beautiful. But she's not my type."

I slowly looked over at Beau, finding his eyes glued to my lips. My stomach fluttered, and my face got all hot.

He suddenly hopped out of the truck.

What just happened? I hopped out, too, but he was already walking away. "Beau?"

"I'm drunk. I need to sleep it off."

"Where are you going?" I called out. He didn't reply, so I went after him for a second time tonight.

I caught up and cut him off on the sidewalk. "It's freezing outside. Just crash on my couch."

"It's not a wise idea."

I rolled my eyes. "I promise not to take advantage of you. Girl Scout's honor." I raised my hand.

Our eyes locked.

"Maybe I'm the one who'll take advantage of *you.*" He slid his arms around my waist and pulled me into him, covering my mouth with his.

Startled by the unexpected kiss, I froze. His lips were warm and soft. He smelled like rum mixed with peppermint candy. *Mmmm... He tastes like the holidays.*

I opened my mouth, inviting him to deepen the kiss. He did. It was a slow, sensual kiss that made my knees wobble and my wobbly bits steam up.

As his mouth and tongue worked against mine, his towering frame pressed against me, warming me from head to toe. I wrapped my arms around him, exploring the hard back muscles under his sweater.

After a few moments, I was dizzy and drunk with lust.

Beau slowly ended the kiss, kneading my lips with his and kissing the corner of my mouth.

He smiled down at me with a seductive grin. "Good night, Meri." He turned to walk away again.

"You're really going to leave?" I asked, breathless.

"I have some business to take care of."

It was one o'clock in the morning. What sort of business could he possibly have?

Flustered beyond belief, I watched Mr. Mixed Signals walk away, refusing to chase after him for a third time tonight. It was one thing to want somebody, but it was another to beg.

He knows where I live.

I went to my apartment and looked out the window at the empty alley, replaying our interactions since we'd met.

So he used to be a spoiled rich kid. I never would've guessed it. *But how could his father turn his back like that?* Not that I knew Beau before all this, but he'd spent a decade of his life living like that guy from *Kung Fu*, a show I'd caught on the old rerun channel. The guy, who was a monk, traveled from place to place, helping others with his mad kung fu skills. Okay, Beau wasn't running around beating people up in the name of justice, but he definitely took his vow of poverty seriously.

I changed into my red flannel bottoms and my tank top with tiny green Christmas trees. While I braided my frizzy hair, I couldn't help wondering what would come next for Beau.

Maybe he's like an outdoor cat now. He'd never be able to settle down into a "normal" life.

I hopped into bed, knowing that I was more fascinated by him than ever.

Suddenly, my door buzzer went off. I got up and pressed the intercom button in the kitchen. "Hello?"

"It's me," said that deep familiar voice.

Beau. My heart lit up, and I did a little dance. "Yes, yes, yes!" I hit the door release to let him in and then rushed to the bathroom to brush my teeth.

By the time I was done, Beau was at my door.

"Hey, you came back," I said, trying to sound casual about it.

"As you can see."

"Are you staying, or are you still worried I might take advantage of you?" I asked coyly.

"I was hoping you might take a few liberties. Though, I am no longer drunk. Only a little tipsy."

"I can work with that." I grabbed him by the

collar of his sweater and pulled him inside, pressing my mouth to his.

He still tasted delicious. Later, I'd have to ask what sort of gum or mouthwash he used.

With our mouths locked, and my body turning into a ball of fire, I pulled off his sweater and tossed it to the floor. His warm hands roamed under my tank top to my waist, gripping me firmly as he bowed his body over me. I ran my hands up to his shoulders and then down his chest, tracing my fingertips along the contours of his pecs and abs.

"How often do you work out at the Y?" I panted between wild, hot kisses.

"A lot."

I reached for the button of his pants. "You're really fit."

"Yes," he panted back, removing my shirt. His hands immediately went to my breasts, cupping and massaging. "You feel so good."

"So do you." His muscles were hard, his skin was soft, and he smelled incredible. "What soap do you use?"

He began walking me back toward the bedroom. "You really want to discuss soap right now?"

"No. No." I pulled down my pajama bottoms, stumbling out of them as we made our way to my bed. His hands were everywhere—my ass, neck and face. We miraculously got to the edge of my bed in one piece.

"I can't get over how good you taste," I said.

"Like candy."

"You too."

"Mint toothpaste."

He pushed me back on the bed and kicked off his boots. He slowly began unbuttoning his jeans and then slid them off.

Commando. Nice.

That was when I saw what he had going on down there. It was thick and long and rock hard. "That is a very big present." I swallowed down the lump in my throat.

"Just wait until you see what it can do."

"Hold that thought." I rolled over and grabbed a condom from my dresser drawer. He snatched it from my hand and rolled it on in two seconds.

He grabbed the sides of my panties and slid them down, taking in the triangle of dark hair between my legs. "That looks delicious."

"Some other time." I grabbed his face and pulled his lips to mine while he settled between my thighs. His body felt so good, so hot. I was aching to have him inside me. "Please promise you're not going to leave again."

He instantly froze. "Meri."

I opened my eyes, locking on his intense gaze. Then he rolled off me.

Oh God. I didn't know why I'd said that out loud. It had been more of a wish than an ask. Wasn't it?

He sat on the edge of the bed for a long moment and then grabbed his jeans, disappearing into the bathroom off the living room.

What just happened? I was wetter than a melting icicle and hotter than a steaming cup of cocoa with tiny marshmallows turning to liquid. I needed him. Genuinely needed him.

The realization slammed into me like a snowball to the face. I'd meant what I'd said just now. I didn't want him to leave. I wanted to get to know him and unravel the mystery of why I felt so drawn to a man who lived a very unconventional life.

I really do like him. I pulled my covers over my body, hugging my white blanket.

I heard the bathroom door open, and then Beau appeared in my bedroom, pulling on his sweater. He sat down on the edge of the bed and began putting on his boots.

"So you're leaving," I said. "Again."

"This was a mistake."

"Why? Because I said I didn't want you to go, like you're doing right now?"

"I told you before that I was content with my life, and I meant it," he replied.

"You mean the wandering from place to place without a home, all to pay penance for something that wasn't actually your fault?"

"I don't expect you to understand." He stood up and stared down at me, a pained look in his blue eyes.

"You're probably right." I got up, dragging my

blanket with me. I grabbed my red robe from my closet and slid it on. "But how could anyone possibly understand when your MO is to push everyone away?" I exhaled sharply. "You're not a hobo or some free bird wandering the planet. You're a chicken shit. That's what you are. Bock, bock. Chicken."

He tilted his head to one side. "Is that supposed to make me feel something?"

"Yeah. Embarrassed. And has it occurred to you that maybe what your dad was waiting for wasn't for his son to live like a hermit crab using a tent as his shell, but to put down some roots and make a difference—to care about someone else more than you care about yourself?"

"I care."

"Oh, do you?" I folded my arms over my chest.

"Tonight I just gave three thousand dollars to my friend who runs the homeless shelter downtown," he said.

That was where he'd gone just now? "Where did you get three thousand dollars?"

"I was working on a crabbing boat the last few weeks," he replied.

"What?"

"Crab. You know, those things with pinchers. People eat them. Working fishing boats is good money."

I shook my head. While I was worrying my ass off, looking everywhere for him—every bus station,

Y, soup kitchen, and park—he was somewhere on the ocean. "So you were fishing."

"I needed a change of scenery to clear my head." He paused for a long moment and then let out a breath. "I was trying to forget I met you."

Suddenly, the anger drained from my body. Now I just felt...sad. "Why? Because of what I said on game night? You know I didn't mean—"

"It's easier that way."

"Beau." I walked up to him, taking his hand. "Probably easier, but so much lonelier."

"Well, it didn't work. I ended up coming right back here as soon as we hit the dock. I was going to stop by tomorrow, but I bumped into your friend Shawna, and she invited me to Friendsgiving. I thought, for one second, that maybe the universe was trying to tell me something. It's why I gave the money away tonight instead of using it to fund my travels to a new place."

"You gave it away so you'd stay? With me?"

He nodded. "Yes, but Meri, it was probably the rum talking and—"

I pushed myself up onto the tips of my toes and kissed him hard. He froze for a moment and then kissed me back.

He felt so right on my lips. I didn't care that he had baggage but didn't own much. He defied everything I'd ever thought comprised the perfect man. And that fact alone mesmerized me. I wanted to fight to keep him here. Yet, all of a sudden, I couldn't stop thinking about something Kay had said: *Give without expectations. Give from the heart.*

It dawned on me that I was in the midst of doing the exact opposite. I wasn't thinking about him at all. I was thinking about what I wanted: for him to stay.

I pulled away, experiencing a moment of clarity unlike any other. "I'll make you a deal. If you feel like staying, then stay. For as long as you need or want. And if you get the itch to travel, then travel. And if you want somewhere to come back to, I'll be here. Unless I move, which I might, but then you'd be welcome there, too. The point is, I'd love for you to stick around, but I don't expect anything from you, Beau," I said softly. "Except your honesty and friendship. I'd also like to know which soap and toothpaste you use because I could probably eat you. You smell that good." I grinned.

"Friends? You want to just be friends?" He clearly didn't believe me.

"I never said that was all I wanted, but in the last ten seconds, I realized that for us to be more, for *me* to be happy, you'd have to want to stick around, but you're not there yet." I shrugged. "Maybe you never will be. Either way, I know I'm a better person for meeting you, and I mean that with all my heart. So if we're friends, and that's all, then I'll take it. But I'm not going to lie just to make you happy."

I felt so proud of myself. I hadn't chucked my needs out the window to make someone else happy, and at the same time, I gave an offer from the heart.

He rubbed his chin. "Friends don't tongue-kiss friends like you do, Meri."

I laughed. "Or like you." I fanned my face. "But I'd be heartbroken if this thing between us went any further and you just upped and disappeared."

He nodded. "I do not want to hurt you."

"Then don't. Friends?" I held out my hand, aching inside. I wanted him. Badly. Just thinking about him being naked on top of me, harder than a jackhammer, made my knees squishy.

He took my hand and gave it a firm shake.

Was this sucking for him, too? If it did, he wasn't letting on. Or maybe this was better for him. No pressure. No strings. I could be a friend to lean on, which he probably needed. Tonight he'd come to the realization that after eight long years, his dad was never going to forgive him. *I'd like to meet his dad and give him a kick in the maracas.*

"I have just one more request," I said.

"What?"

"Will you please stay the night? On the couch? It's late. You're on the other side of drunk, and I'm exhausted. If you go, I'll just sit here worrying about where you're staying, feeling like I didn't try hard enough to convince you that I really meant what I said. I'm here for you. And I think you are better than you know—just the type of guy a girl like me would do anything for, including depriving herself of a hard, steamy bang." I blinked. "I don't know why I said that. Sorry."

"I forgot all my things in Shawna's car, but I'll stay. If it makes you feel better."

"I can text her and ask if she can drop your stuff off tomorrow." I clapped. "I'm just going to go and see if I still have some of Mike's things in the closet."

"Mike?"

"My ex. He left me due to irreconcilable differences."

"What type?" he asked.

"I tend to go a little overboard for Christmas—if you can tell. I think he looked down on me for it."

Beau's eyes looked around my crazy apartment. "Please don't ever stop." His voice was everything sincere.

I bobbed my head, acknowledging his words. "Well, I guess there comes a point when we all have to accept reality. Mine is that I can't make everyone happy." I let go of a breath. "I'll go see if I can dig out those clothes for you."

"No. I'm good," he said.

"Okay. Night, Beau."

"Night, Meri. Sweet dreams."

"Thanks," I said, knowing I'd have anything but.

Tonight had been filled with so many surprises, from Kay convincing me to go to Friendsgiving, to Shawna forgiving me, to Beau showing up and my heart being overcome with relief to see him. Then he left and came back again, almost rocking my Christmas stocking. Now I was trying to bury some serious feelings. All because I genuinely cared about what happened to this man.

What a freaking night. I went to my room, closed the door, and got out my favorite stationery with the little reindeers around the edges. I needed some way to let it all out—this strange amalgamation of lust and sadness mixed with a deep, gnawing hope to see Beau happy, to find joy in his life again. It warmed my heart to imagine him free of his past even if the price of helping him was only being friends—not my first choice.

If it were up to me, he'd stay, and we'd see where this thing between us could go. Because I did want him. Just not like this. He was wrestling with some pretty difficult feelings that made him live like a fugitive.

I was wrestling with my own feelings, too, but I knew I'd be fine no matter what. I had friends and family. I had people to lean on. *Unconditional love…*

Yes. That was my wish for Beau. To find what I had. To know that whatever happened in life, he would be loved.

Dear Santa,

I know I'm late writing you, but maybe it's by design. Because this year, I have a very special request. It's not for me, but for—

I paused and exhaled.

—a friend. His name is Beau, and he is a wonderful person...

CHAPTER FIFTEEN

The next morning, I expected to wake up alone, my wanderer gone in search of something to fill the gaping hole in his heart. But to my utter joy, I found Beau in my kitchen, making pancakes. The entire apartment smelled like buttery carbs, cinnamon, and maple syrup.

"Hi," I said, walking on eggshells, afraid I might wake up from this dream.

"Hey. I made coffee. Breakfast will be ready soon."

I smiled, quietly melting. He'd stayed. He'd fucking stayed. "Can I help?"

"You can set the table?"

A sit-down breakfast. "Sure." I went to the corner of my small living room and pulled my little table away from the wall. I didn't eat here much, since it was usually only me, but it was absolutely an occasion to bust out the four leaves.

I got everything ready, and Beau came out with the biggest stack of hotcakes I'd ever seen. He quickly returned with coffee, butter, and syrup.

I took a sip from my mug, tasting an explosion

of dark, nutty goodness. "Did you buy this?"

"I couldn't sleep, so I walked to the store and got a few things. Oh, and Shawna dropped my stuff off, too. I ran into her outside."

I bet she hit on him again, too. *Grrr...* I tamped down my ridiculous jealousy. "Thank you. This coffee is great."

"I blended it myself—espresso beans with Kona. I added some cocoa extract and a drop of hazelnut."

"Wow." I took another sip. "It's amazing."

"Try my pancakes. They're made with almond flour and coconut for texture and flavor."

"Where did you learn to cook?"

"My mother. Baking was mandatory at our house."

"I love baking," I said. "But my specialty is cookies."

"Bread is baked for the stomach, but cookies are baked from the heart—as my mother used to say."

"How long ago did she pass away?"

He took a bite of his food, hesitating to answer. "About eleven years ago."

That would have been before the factory fire. "I'm really sorry. It must've been hard. Do you have any siblings?"

"I do not."

"Then even harder." He'd had to go through it with his grieving father.

"She was the heart of our family, but she lives on in here." He pointed to his chest.

"And here." I took a bite of my pancakes and rolled my eyes in bliss. They were fluffy and chewy with hints of almond. "So good." I chewed and swallowed. "Did she teach you *this* recipe?"

"Yes."

"I think she and I would've gotten along." I smiled and took another bite, thinking about what I'd just learned. "Do you think her death had anything to do with why your father is keeping you away?"

He shrugged. "I do not know. Why?"

"It's just that people deal with loss in different ways, yanno? Maybe he was afraid of losing you, too, so he did all this to push you away."

Beau laughed. "You don't know my father. All he cares about is making toys. To him, other people's happiness is everything. The rest of us be damned."

I winced. That was nothing like my father. Our family's happiness was everything to him.

"Let's change subjects," Beau said.

Beau was right. I was trying too hard to fix something that wasn't mine to fix. I needed to be a friend not a buttinski. "Are you staying for lunch?"

He gave me a look. "Have you seen the amount of pancakes on our plates? I doubt I'll be hungry for hours."

"Okay, what about dinner? Just so I can plan what we'll eat. No pressure or anything."

He smiled, flashing a charming smile my way. "I

decided to stay a few days."

"Wow. Look at you not hoboing away." I beamed at him. "I'm proud of you."

"Don't be. I just decided to take a break—let my new situation soak in."

Now I was extra proud of him.

"Stop gloating," he said, still smiling.

"What?" I looked down at my plate and chewed with a grin.

"There's a tree lighting tonight downtown. Would you like to go?"

"Will hot chocolate be involved?" I asked.

"Well, you wanted to have dinner together, right?"

Cocoa for dinner. "I'm in." I just had to be careful. He planned to split in a few days, and that would be that. I might never see him again. *One meal at a time, Meri. Just enjoy today.*

༄ ༅

That evening, Beau and I walked along the plaza, sipping dinner and waiting for the tree-lighting ceremony to start. Families, groups of friends, and couples were everywhere, bundled up in winter jackets and enjoying the music piping from the band near the tree.

Beau had on his thick black parka. I wore my trusty red coat.

"I've never come to this," I said. "Thanks for the

invite."

"Really? I figured this was an annual tradition for you."

"Nope. I'm usually too busy preparing for my big holiday bash."

"So why aren't you now?" he asked.

"I've decided not to throw my party this year."

"Why?" he asked.

"I don't know. I guess I'm just not feeling it." Also, there was a certain person occupying my thoughts. "And honestly, I'm not sure my friends really enjoyed it. Not like I thought, anyway."

"I find that hard to believe. I can see all the energy you put into decorating."

"I do." I laughed. Suddenly, my phone buzzed. I pulled it from my pocket. It was Kay. "Hey, what's up?"

"Meri, I completely forgot," her voice sounded panicked, "but I volunteered to help my mom host the annual Sock and Sip next Sunday." The Sock and Sip was an auction back in my hometown. For the party, people donated lots of wine and snacks, and they usually booked a DJ for dancing. But most importantly, everyone donated Christmas stockings filled with everything from beauty supplies to candy and X-rated stuff for the adults, all to auction off. Some even gave away vacations. All the money went to the local foodbank for Christmas.

"And?" I said.

"I can't go. I have a big client to show around

early the next day, and I'll be dead if I try to drive back to the city after the auction. You know how late that thing goes. Can you do it?"

"Kay, it's a five-hour drive to get there."

"But you don't have to rush home. You booked time off, right?" she asked.

In addition to taking off the week after Christmas, I always took vacation time around the beginning of December to finish wrapping gifts and to do party prep. Of course, this year, I wasn't doing any of that, but I hadn't told anyone but Beau.

"Please, Meri. You know how my mom gets, and my dad is useless for this stuff. You've done the event twice before, and you're so organized." Kay's parents were the kindest people on the planet, but their laid-back hippy ways weren't exactly the best for organizing charity events like this one. The auction was incredibly fun, but pure chaos. Especially after people got a few drinks in them and started taking off their socks, throwing them around the room. It was weird, but funny.

"What about your sister or one of her friends?" I suggested.

"My sister can't be around food smells right now, and none of her friends are available."

"Ugh. Sure, I suppose I can do it." So I'd take two trips home this December. Not the end of the world.

"Thank you!" She sighed with relief. "You're the best. Oh, I almost forgot. What happened with

Beau? Girl, he's smokin' hot! The ladies at Friendsgiving couldn't stop going on about him. I swear there were little puddles all over the chairs."

"Ew!"

"Just sayin'," she laughed, "if things don't work out with Lick, Beau can park his big tent inside my lady garden—"

"Bye, Kay." I ended the call.

"Everything all right?" Beau asked.

Besides the fact my friends all want you? "I have to drive home next weekend to help Kay's mom with a charity thing. You're welcome to come, but I'll be staying with my parents."

He gave me a look.

"I know. Meeting my folks is a lot. Just forget I asked."

"No, I'd love to meet them." He smirked. "I want to see who's responsible for making you—"

"Such a mess?"

"Such a persistent woman."

I stared at his handsome face for a long moment. I loved looking at him—those intense, sparkling blue eyes, those soft lips, and thick dark lashes. He *was* edible.

Suddenly, the announcement went over the plaza's loudspeakers. They were about to light the tree. Both Beau and I turned to face it, holding our warm cups of cocoa. I wanted to be holding something completely different, attached to his body.

"Persistent, huh?" I smiled, staring up at the big

dark tree. Maybe that was Beau's way of saying I shouldn't give up on him. *Or he was just trying to pay a compliment, you big dork.*

"You convinced me to stay last night, didn't you?" he said.

I had. And now he'd be coming home to meet my parents, and I didn't know what any of it meant. *Just friends. Just friends. Just friends…*

CHAPTER SIXTEEN

The rest of the evening with Beau was, well, *incredible*. Like, as in vibing-on-all-levels kind of incredible.

After the tree-lighting ceremony, we did a little shopping before the department store closed to get him some clothes. He paid for everything with money he'd kept from crabbing, which wasn't much but enough for jeans, tees, and socks. No undies.

Thank you, god of fantasies. The commando memories would live on.

One thing I noticed, though, was that Beau had the most incredible luck. He'd had a list of everything he needed to buy, and there they were, waiting for him on a shelf in the store. No exaggeration. The button-fly jeans he wanted were right next to a navy blue T-shirt and a white sweater, both on his list. In his size. In the sock aisle. Next to a bag of socks also on his list. *What luck.*

"I wish I could get that lucky when I shop," I'd said. "Would save tons of time."

He'd tapped the side of his head. "It's all in here."

Yeah, sure. I'd tried the whole manifestation thing. Never worked. "Can you do my shopping from now on? Make sure there's a bag of cash on my list, wuddja?"

He'd laughed. "Who needs money when the universe provides?"

"Someone is in a very optimistic mood tonight." I'd smiled, thinking how good it felt to see him like this.

After, we went back to my place, and he made bow-tie pasta from a recipe he'd learned growing up. We laughed, drank wine, and told each other embarrassing childhood stories. But the biggest surprise of the evening? The thing that rattled me down to the core? I found out how much we had in common:

Loved holiday music from the 1950s.

Favorite colors: red and green.

Hated black licorice.

Secretly liked rom-coms and true crime, but only cried for movies when the hero or heroine broke free of their past.

Spicy food, yes.

Sweets only during the holidays.

Always felt guilty when we had over fifty items in our carts because the people behind us had to wait so long for their turn.

We. Both. Loved. Christmas.

And puppies. Couldn't walk past one without petting their furry little faces. Cats were cool, but their independent, curious nature made us worry too much.

Most of all, Beau and I discovered that we both grew up feeling restless all the time, like a cosmic itch we couldn't scratch. It used to drive my parents crazy when I was a child because all I wanted to do was run around, exploring or taking things apart and putting them back together again. I was bad at that last part.

I also read a lot, but they were always "practical" books, like how a rocket ship worked. Sometimes I dug holes in search of treasure, or I panned for gold in the backyard pond. Then one day, I got into crafting Christmas decorations and never stopped.

Beau was still learning to deal with his "wild energy," still as restless as ever. Which was the very reason I convinced myself that our similarities were *not* a sign. I'd only be setting myself up for disappointment to fall for someone like him, and I knew it.

The only problem now was that the entire evening, Beau kept smiling, and when he did, his face lit up in a display that was impossible not to stare at. His dark hair seemed to shine a little more, and that beard he'd shaved off on Halloween was now a thick carpet of black. Together, they framed his face like a picture of radiant joy.

Was it because someone finally believed in him or I'd offered unconditional friendship? I didn't know, but one thing was becoming clear: Beau was probably *not* good friend material for me. He was hot, steamy, dream material.

Case in point: last night I woke up to him shaking me. He'd said that I was making sounds like an alley cat with a broken leg. *Reywrrr! Reywrrr!*

"I guess I was having a nightmare," I'd said. But really, I'd been dreaming of riding him cowgirl style on a sleigh. There were lights all around us, and people were cheering as we slushed on by like a portable winter porn movie.

Thankfully, Beau left early this morning, saying that he had to "take care of more business," which gave me the opportunity to cool off. Aka flick one out. Seriously, I didn't know how much more *friendship* I could take, and it had been less than twenty-four hours.

At least tomorrow I could go to work and let numbers distract me until my eyes crossed.

With laundry done and my apartment dusted and vacuumed, Sunday night rolled around, but there was no sign of Beau. He didn't have a cell, so there was no way to call and make sure he was okay.

Convincing myself I was being silly for worrying about a man who'd lived as a proud, self-sufficient hobo for ten years, I brushed my teeth, got into my PJs, and tucked myself into bed. But as I tossed and turned, my dark thoughts wouldn't let up.

What if something had finally happened to him? He could be in a ditch, bleeding or choking on a sandwich.

"Dammit." I got up, slid on my tennis shoes and coat, and grabbed my purse. I got into my truck and drove around, hitting the main streets around my neighborhood.

No sign of him.

I felt so worried, I didn't even enjoy the lights, which were spectacular during the holidays. The homeowners on my street, Peppermint Street, always went all out, decorating the fronts of their houses and trees. It was tradition.

After over an hour, I finally gave up. I had work in the morning, so I'd simply need to trust that Beau could take care of himself.

On the way inside my building, I bumped into Jason going out the front door.

"Haven't seen you around in a while," he said. "Everything okay?"

"Oh. Yeah. It's just that I have a friend staying with me, and he hasn't come back yet. Was a little worried, so took a spin around the block." *Or ten spins.*

"A friend, huh?" He wiggled his brows. "Does *he* have a name?"

I felt embarrassed to admit who the friend was—*I mean, Tent Guy. Hello*—but my worry for Beau superseded my discomfort over being judged. "You remember the man in the red tent?"

"Doesn't ring a bell. Why?"

Huh? Jason was the one who shunned me the first time I saw Beau and wanted him removed. On the other hand, the last time Jason and I spoke, he only recalled seeing Beau just the once despite the fact that Beau had stuck around for weeks. Still, it was odd that he didn't remember Beau at all.

"Are you sure you don't remember him?" I pushed. "I complained about a tent right next to the dumpster."

Jason wiggled his lips from side to side. "Ohhh...that guy. Wait, he's your *friend*?" Jason chuckled.

"Don't be rude. He's a really nice person."

"Hey, to each their own," he said. "I just never pegged you for the type of woman who went for older men."

"Older? He's my age."

Jason gave me a look like I was insane. "Maybe we're talking about two different people. The guy I saw was in his late sixties. Kind of thick in the middle. Long white beard."

I laughed. "That's definitely not Beau."

"Hmm. Well, I'll keep an eye out for a lost guy about your age."

"Thanks. Night, Jason."

"Night."

I went up to my place, scratching my head. Maybe Beau had let some old guy crash in his tent. It wouldn't be entirely out of character to help a stranger.

I snuggled under my covers and finally drifted off to sleep.

∽ ∾

The next morning, I woke up to an empty apartment. No nutty, dark coffee. No delicious smell of pancakes. And no Beau.

I was officially worried, but I had to be at work. There was a big insurance quote due for a developer planning to build a sprawling, three-hundred-home development. My bosses would not be happy if I turned in my risk assessment late.

I rushed to get dressed and headed for the door. Two steps outside, I bumped into Beau coming up the walkway. I didn't know whether to be relieved or furious. *Both. Definitely both.*

"What happened to you?" I asked calmly.

He rubbed the back of his messy dark hair. "I stopped by the shelter yesterday and ended up helping out with some repairs in their kitchen. After that, I was walking back here and saw a For Hire sign in a window. I applied, and they gave me a job right on the spot."

What luck. "Seriously? Doing what?"

"Baking, which you know I love. Though, I've been doing it all night. They had a big cookie order for a party."

"That's great, Beau. Congratulations," I said tightly, trying not to be mad. "So, is this a full-time gig?" If yes, it meant he planned to stick around. That would be fantastic!

"Could be. Right now, I'm seasonal and part-time."

Seasonal was okay, too—a step in the right direction.

He added, "I hope you don't mind me staying with you a few more days?"

Oh, definitely I minded. Seeing his gorgeous face would be torture, but this was what he needed to sort out his life. "You can stay as long as you like."

"I actually found a room for rent. I can move in as early as next week."

I blinked. This was incredible news. I mean, renting a room was a commitment to stay put. At least for a while. He just wouldn't be doing it with me.

I masked the disappointment stirring in my chest. "It's all happening so fast. I'm really happy for you."

"You have *no* idea how fast," he muttered. "It is all very unexpected."

"Sorry?"

"I meant—you have already been so generous, and I cannot rely on you forever. An independent woman like you needs her space to...embrace big life changes. Yes?"

Why did I feel like Beau was speaking in code? "I guess so?"

"Exactly." His eyes moved to my lips.

Feeling self-aware, I licked them and then regretted it. I didn't want him to think I was, well, asking him to kiss me, even if right now the only thing I wanted was to throw my arms around the man and shove my tongue down his throat.

"Like I said, I'm here for you." I smiled warmly. "I just have one ask: could you let me know you're all right next time?"

He beamed down at me. "Were you worried all night?"

Yes, and I wasted a gallon of gas driving around looking for you in a ditch. "A little." Suddenly, I remembered the time. "Oh, hey, I have to get to work. Will I see you tonight?"

"I have to be at the bakery around six today."

In other words, he'd be gone before I got home.

"Oh." My heart sank a little farther.

"But Meri," he added sternly, "you do not have to lose sleep over me. I'm fairly resilient at this point in my life. Nothing to worry about."

I got that he had some serious street smarts, but… "I care about you, so the worrying comes with the territory."

He stepped in closer, like he maybe wanted to kiss me, but then he stopped himself. "I'll let you get going. See you tomorrow morning maybe."

"Sure." I headed for my truck, feeling completely sunk. I'd hardly get to see him, and then he'd be moving out on his own. At least I'd get to spend time with him this weekend.

"Hey," he said as I walked away, "I forgot to mention I have to work this weekend, so I can't go with you. I hope you don't mind."

Crap. My stomach filled with concrete blocks made of solid disappointment.

Maybe it was all for the best. We were just friends, after all. Not lovers. Not a couple. Not anything more than two people who'd met next to a dumpster in an alley and almost had unforgettable sex.

"No worries!" I waved over my shoulder. "You can always come home with me for Christmas."

I winced as I kept walking to my truck. I'd sounded so desperate. *There's always Christmas, Beau. Blah, blah, blah,* I mocked myself. *I'm not planning your future like a sad, lonely woman.*

The worst part was that he'd said nothing in return. And why should he? I'd friend-zoned him, and he'd friend-zoned me right back.

But what choice did I have? He was who he was—a man who'd grown accustomed to being a leaf in the wind—and I didn't want to love someone who'd break my heart. All that aside, I'd wanted to see him happy and start building a life for himself. Now he was happy. Or, at least, he was taking steps to get there.

So then why was I feeling miserable all of a sudden? Maybe because each step he took led further away from me.

CHAPTER SEVENTEEN

"Meri, got any plans tonight?" Shawna asked at the end of the day Friday. "We're all going to a holiday karaoke thing near the marina. You can bring Beau if you want."

I barely looked at her, feeling glummer than ever. "I have to drive to my folks' place tonight, remember?" In fact, I needed to leave right about now if I wanted to make it before the next snowstorm rolled in tonight.

"I completely forgot. Is Beau going with you?" she asked.

I wish. "No, he has to work this weekend. He got a job baking."

"I love a Black man who can bake." She paused. "Or any man who can cook, honestly. Queen Shawna doesn't discriminate when it comes to good food."

I frowned at her strange comment. "Well, Beau is a great cook for sure."

"Meri, why do you sound like someone kicked you in the lady hump? You've been dragging your saggy, skinny ass around the office all week."

I grabbed my purse and started packing up for the day. "My ass is fat, but thanks for the compliment. And I'm fine," I said in a miserable not-fine voice.

"Are you? Because you haven't brought any baked goods to the office this week, and you're usually swinging into high gear by now, determined to plump us all up by Christmas. And I still haven't received my invite for your party."

I sighed. "Yeah. I'm not throwing one this year."

Shawna's mouth fell open. "Now I know something's up."

"I don't want to talk about it," I muttered.

"Okay, but if it's a question of help or anything like that, all you have to do is ask. I know you've been working like crazy lately, so—"

"No." I shook my head. "It's not that. I just…don't have the motivation this year."

"But you're Miss *Ing*. Never stops cook*ing*, bak*ing*, plann*ing*, decorat*ing*…"

"Well, I recently learned that my enthusiasm for *ing*ing isn't actually shared by everyone."

"I can't speak for your other friends, but I always look forward to crazy Christmas at Meri's."

"Shawna, even you said the other day that all I ask of you as a friend is to show up at my party once a year."

"It's true. You're very low maintenance."

"But that's my point. My party shouldn't be a

chore." I grabbed my laptop and shoved it in my bag. "It's supposed to be a gift—something you *get* to do instead of *having* to do."

I knew I came off sounding like I was having a pity party for one, and maybe I was, but the joy of Christmas had been zapped right out of me this year. Then I'd met Beau and…and…

Started using him as a distraction. But the truth was that maybe it was time to move on and start focusing on other things. *Things other than Christmas and Beau.*

I could begin by spending time figuring out what I really wanted to do with the rest of my life. One by one, my friends were getting married and having kids. Even Kay's little sister had busted out an entire family.

What did I have?

A storage locker filled with decorations for a house I didn't own, for a family I didn't have and never would if I didn't stop my obsession for a very unavailable man.

What am I doing? Who did I think I was, pretending to rescue Beau? He was the last person who needed saving. The guy literally snapped his fingers and got a job and a place to stay. He'd taken care of himself for years with zero support. He was the least needy person I'd ever met. And here I was running around thinking I needed to save *him*.

"I'm really sorry if I ever made you feel that way," said Shawna. "I love your party, and if you change your mind about throwing it, just say the word. I'll clean, bring supplies, and do whatever you need help with. Except cooking. I suck at that. But your hot Black baker friend can whip us up some treats."

I gave her a look. "What baker?"

She laughed. "Beau. Hello? You know, the guy who's been staying with you."

"Shawna...but he's..." I was about to say he wasn't Black, but I bit my tongue. Maybe she wasn't well. And if not, she needed help. The sort I couldn't give her.

I'd have to contact her sister on the way home.

"But he's what?" she asked.

"I was going to say that he's probably not sticking around much longer. He doesn't stay in one place very long."

"It's the season for wishing, though. Right?"

"Right. See you when I get back." I'd be off next week. "And have fun tonight." I got my things and left.

༄ ༅

The entire drive home, I couldn't stop thinking about Shawna. It was one thing to forget a name or not recall someone's eye color, but she couldn't remember what Beau looked like. I was genuinely concerned.

I found Egypt's profile online and sent her a

DM, telling her I needed to talk. I gave her my number and let her know I'd be on the road, driving to my parents', so if I didn't answer, to leave a message. The reception wasn't always great on those mountain roads.

I pulled up to my building, planning to run in, grab my suitcase and snow chains, and then hit the road. With luck, I'd beat the storm by an hour.

I entered the building, finding Jason sweeping the top of the staircase. There were little pieces of white fluff everywhere.

"Mrs. Larson buy a flocked tree again?" I asked.

"I keep telling her to get a regular tree and do that stuff inside her own place, but she never listens. Or cleans up. By the way, I just saw that old guy go into your place."

I stopped on the first step with my keys in my hand. "What old guy?"

"The one you asked me about the other day."

"No, I asked about my friend—the one who's my age."

He shook his head. "No, you didn't. You asked if I'd seen a man with a long white beard."

Was everyone losing their minds? "Is he in my place right now?"

Jason nodded.

"And you're one hundred percent positive he didn't go into Mrs. Larson's apartment?" Could be a friend of hers.

"Yeah."

"Errr…" I didn't believe him. I took the stairs, sailing past Jason, who followed me to my door.

"I would've stopped him, but he said he was your guest," Jason added. "He had a key and everything."

I shoved my key in the door, but it was already unlocked. I opened the door slowly and peeked inside my living room.

"Hello?" I heard the shower running, so I went to the door and knocked. "Hello?"

"Hey, Meri. I'll be out in a sec," Beau called out.

I looked at Jason and then the door. Jason then door.

"Umm…it's my friend's dad. He *loves* showering at my place. I forgot he was coming," I said, just so Jason wouldn't worry. But it was definitely Beau in there.

He arched a brow. "Ohhh-kaaay." Jason headed out to the hallway.

"Thanks for keeping an eye on things. See you later." I gave him a little wave, and Jason closed the door behind him. A few moments later, Beau came out of the shower with a towel around his waist. His wet muscular abs glistened like twinkling white lights, hypnotizing me.

Goddamn, he's so sexy.

"Meri?" Beau snapped his fingers, grinning. My drooling probably amused him.

"Oh, uh…" I pointed toward the front door.

"My downstairs neighbor said he saw some old guy coming in here."

"Old guy?"

"Yeah, with a white beard."

Beau suddenly started acting strange—avoiding eye contact, serious expression. "It's just me in here." He grabbed some clothes from his red duffel bag next to the couch.

"What's going on?" I asked.

"Nothing."

"If you have someone here, you can tell me," I said.

"But I don't."

"Jason saw the same man hanging around your tent once, too, so clearly he's a friend of yours." I went to the hall closet and checked inside.

"What are you doing?" Beau asked.

I went to my bedroom and checked the other closet. There was nothing but clothes. I got on my knees and looked under my bed.

"Meri," Beau barked.

I looked up at him. "Why are you lying to me? I know someone's here."

"There's no one."

"Did they go out the fire escape?" I got to my feet and looked out the window.

"You don't have a fire escape," he said.

"Good point, but why are you lying to me?" The idea of it triggered me on every level. I'd trusted a person I didn't know and allowed them into my home. I'd started to care about him deeply, too. The thought of being lied to by him made me feel like the world's biggest sucker.

"I'm not lying," he said firmly.

We locked gazes for a long moment. My head was spinning, and my stomach was telling me to open my eyes. Something was off about this entire situation.

"Meri," he said, breaking the silence, "I need to dress and get to work, but—"

"Maybe letting you stay here was a bad idea. I don't even know you, Beau."

His blue eyes filled with a subtle pain. "Funny. I was about to say that you know me better than anyone, and that our friendship means everything to me. I wouldn't ruin it by lying to you over nothing."

"That's the thing; maybe it isn't nothing." Maybe he was lying for a much bigger reason. At the end of the day, I did not know this man. "I have to hit the road, but please be gone by the time I get back." I'd return on Monday, which left him plenty of time to pitch a tent or make other arrangements.

"Meri, I—"

"Stop, okay?" I grabbed my packed suitcase from the corner. "I know you're lying. I just don't know why, and frankly, it doesn't matter."

"You mean our friendship doesn't matter," he said bitterly.

"I never should've meddled in your life. You

were happy doing your camping thing, wandering the globe, being a free bird. You just happened to come along at a time in my life when everything's on the verge of changing. I probably just used you to avoid facing the fact I'm turning thirty on Christmas, and I have nothing to show for it."

"Your birthday is on Christmas?"

"Yes, and I throw myself a big party every year to celebrate, claiming it's for Christmas because I don't want presents or cake. I just enjoy having my friends around. But they're all starting to move on, and I'm here trying to fix a hobo instead of focusing on the one person who really needs my attention. Me."

"So no one knows it's your birthday?"

Kay knew, and she respected the fact that I didn't celebrate the day like everyone else. Why would I when the only thing people wanted to do was focus on the holidays, which I happened to love, too? So it was a win-win. But that wasn't the point. "Beau, I have to go, but I wish you all the luck in the world. Not that you need it." Just like he never needed me. Just like my friends never needed my party. It was time for me to grow up and start getting honest with myself.

I headed for the door and closed it.

As I went outside, lugging my stuff, I spotted a big white van parked out front. The driver—who wore the same red uniform and hat—came rushing up the walkway, carrying a white box with a red bow.

"Excuse me. Is Beau Starling here? I have another package for him," said the man.

"Sure. He's in apartment four. Just knock." I let the man inside the building and continued on my way.

I knew it was another letter from Beau's dad, but it wasn't my business any longer.

CHAPTER EIGHTEEN

"I'm sorry you're feeling so down about your party and everything else, sweetie," said my mom the next morning over coffee in the breakfast nook with the big window overlooking the front yard. Outside, the pine trees were covered in a blanket of snow, and the driveway was completely hidden. If I'd arrived ten minutes later last night, my truck wouldn't have made it since I'd forgotten my snow chains.

My mom went on, "But no matter what, we always bake you a cake. Plus your brothers and everyone else will be here to celebrate."

They were never here to celebrate my birthday. They came to my folks' house for Christmas.

"It's not the same when everyone gets to open gifts on your birthday and cake is the last thing anyone wants." My mom prepared everything from spicy tamales and sweet pies to roasted lamb and herbed potatoes. No one had room for cake after all that, not even me.

"I tried to squeeze you out early," she said, "but baby Jesus just wasn't having it. By the way, did you see the new one I put in the manger outside? It has

LED lights so you can change his color. Blue, green, or even orange."

Weird. "Sounds great, Mom. Bet it goes great with all the decorations." The house had lights in every tree along the driveway, lights on the roof, lights around the windows, and more lights on every inch of the front porch. At night, it reminded me of a bright spaceship about to take off. With a manger and baby Jesus, of course. *Now in blue, green, or orange.*

"I'll show you tonight after your father gets home. We can make a fire, drink cocoa, and watch a movie." My dad was out helping a neighbor with a fallen tree.

"That sounds great," I said, "but I plan to sleep." Nothing like coming home to recover from the chaos of adulting and failing at life.

"Sure you don't want anything for breakfast?" she asked. "Some pancakes?"

Pancakes instantly made me think of Beau. I still couldn't get over how he'd lied to me. Then again, what was I thinking? I'd let a stranger into my life, into my home, and into my erogenous zones. I'd somehow talked myself into believing it was all perfectly normal.

"Thanks, but I'm good," I said. "I think I'll head over to the community center and help Libby set up." Libby was Kay's mom, and since I'd come a day early to beat the storm, I had time to kill. "But let me know if you need anything from the store. I can swing by on my way back."

"Sounds good, honey."

I went to take a shower and prepare for the day. At least the snow had eased up, but I'd have to drive mom's SUV.

I went to my old room, which hadn't changed much since I went away to college, including the pink carpet. There were still photos of me and Kay on my corkboard, the two of us with our goofy smiles and bad hair. There was a picture of my friend group all sitting around a picnic table, wearing cowboy hats for pioneer day. There was even a drawing from art class of my dream house—the one with the red barn.

"Where did you go, Meri?" I said to myself. I'd had so many plans, so many dreams. I'd wanted to travel and see the world, maybe open my own business and eventually fall in love. Instead, I got a job in the city after college, working in insurance. How boring. I'd been stuck there ever since.

I really did need a change. Or more accurately stated, I needed to find myself again.

§

That evening, I pulled up to my parents' Christmas spaceship, noting a big white truck in the driveway. Maybe it was a friend of theirs who'd come to see the blue baby.

Me? I had a date with a long hot bath. I was

sore and tired after cleaning all the chairs and tables for tomorrow's auction. It was a good thing I'd showed up to the community center because Libby didn't even have a list of tasks. We still had the lights to set up, the bar to organize, and the sound system to check for the live auction and DJ. We'd also have to ensure the auction ran smoothly—cataloging each stocking and collecting the money from the bid winners.

I trudged through the snow toward the porch, feeling wiped out. Just then, a man in a bright red coat slid from the truck. He had a long white beard and white hair. His intense blue eyes seemed familiar somehow.

"Are you Meri?" he asked, his voice baritone and unfriendly.

I stopped five feet away. "Yes. And you are?"

"Beau's father."

The backstabbing, jerk-face father? This was unexpected, not to mention strange.

"He's not here." Then again, he would know that since he'd delivered a package to Beau yesterday. "What do you want?"

"Beau refused to take the keys."

I arched a brow. "Keys?"

"I know he told you about my factory. I've asked him to take charge of her before I retire in a few weeks."

All right. So apparently his father changed his mind about things. Why? Not sure. Didn't care.

"This has nothing to do with me."

The man shook a gloved finger at me. "It has everything to do with you. But, Meri, he would be making a very big mistake to turn his back on everything now."

I blinked. "You mean like you turned your back on him for the last ten years?"

Indignation sparked in the man's intense eyes. "I *never* turned my back on him. He simply was not ready." The man ran a hand through his thick white hair. "I wasn't sure he ever would be, and now that he is, he refuses to take over."

I had no clue what to say. "I'm very sorry you drove all this way, Mr. Starling, but I can't help—"

"He says he won't leave you. He's heck-bent on making things right."

Heck-bent? "There's nothing to make right. Not with me, anyway, so—"

"Meri." He took two steps closer and stared deeply into my eyes, making my insides twist with fear. There was something very off about this man. Aggressive. Authoritative. Yet kind of cute. "You are a good girl, but just because you have friends in high places does not mean I cannot punish you for defying me. Mark my words, if you stand in my son's way, it will not only ruin his life, but the lives of many others, including yours and your family's. Is that what you want? Because once you get on my naughty list, you will never come off it."

Naughty list? Was this guy for real?

The man pulled a set of gold keys from his coat pocket. "Make him take the keys, Meri. Do whatever you must, but he has to take them before Christmas. Understand?"

I nodded slowly, completely freaking the fuck out. Beau's dad was a crazy shit. First, for showing up out of the blue like this. Second, for making demands when he didn't know me. Third, for threatening me and my family.

"You need to leave."

"That factory is his destiny," the man growled. "Not some common, spiritless half-wit like you."

"Wow... Thankfully, the apple *does* fall far from the tree." Beau would never speak to me like that.

The man got into his truck and backed out of the driveway, disappearing down the road.

"Jesus. What a—"

My phone rang in my purse. I slid it out, not realizing my hands were shaking. "He-hello?"

"Hey, Meri. Sorry I didn't call sooner, but I just got your message," said a female voice.

"Who is this?" I asked.

"Egypt. You asked me to call. What's going on?"

I took a second, trying to unscramble my head from that toxic interaction with Beau's dad. I felt light-headed, and the air all around me smelled funny, like spices. I glanced down at the keys in my hand, my head whirring like a blender. A slideshow began flipping through my mind of all the oddities from the past few months: Beau, his luck, the fact that people couldn't remember him, my inexplicable attraction to a man camping next to garbage...

My heart was thumping, and my brain began throbbing, like they were both trying to tell me something.

"Meri! You there?" Egypt said.

"Hey, I know this is a really strange question, but what celebrity does Beau look like?"

"You had me call for that? Is this a joke?" she snapped.

"It's to settle an argument with Shawna." I couldn't come up with a better explanation.

"Jeez, girl. I thought it was an emergency. You scared the shit out of me, and not in a fun way. I'm on that horror-cation, and I just watched an evil elf decapitate a snowman."

So wrong. "Which celebrity!" I barked.

"I don't know!" she barked back. "Maybe Henry Golding?"

My hand with the phone dropped to my side. Jason saw a man that looked like Beau's dad, Shawna saw a Black guy, and Egypt saw the lead actor from *Crazy Rich Asians*.

I looked over my shoulder at the street where the white truck had just disappeared. *What the fuck is going on?*

"I gotta go." I disconnected with Egypt and called my apartment, hoping Beau would answer, but it went to voicemail.

Of course, he'd be working.

I rushed inside and headed to my room, putting the gold keys in my desk drawer before pulling out my laptop. I did a quick search of every bakery in my neighborhood in the city. I came up with six.

I called the first two, but no one answered since it was after hours. But on the third one, I got a woman.

"Hi, hello. Is there a Beau Starling working there?"

"Uh, yes. He's in the back."

"Can I talk to him, please? Tell him it's Meri. It's an emergency," I said, frantically pacing my pink carpet.

"Just a sec."

After a long moment, Beau came on the line. "Meri?"

"Beau! What the *freak* is happening?" *Why did I say freak? I meant fuck!* "Some man just showed up to my parents', claiming to be your dad. He gave me a set of keys and threatened me."

"Son of a snowman."

"Beau, don't get cute with me. What's going on?" I yelled. "Why does Shawna think you're Black? Why does her sister think you're Asian? What is this?"

He whooshed out a long breath. "I think you know what this is."

"No, I freaking don't." *Fucking! Fucking don't. Why is my mouth not working?*

"I cannot explain right now, but when you return, we can sit down, and I will—"

"I'm *not* coming back. I don't feel safe around you." I started tearing up. None of this made any sense.

"Please do not say that, Meri. I would never hurt you."

"What about your dad, huh? What is he? Drug trafficker? Mafia? One of those weird cult members who turns everyone into eunuchs?" Very uncool. Penises were awesome.

"No. He's not dangerous. Not the way you mean, anyway."

"Oh, great. But he *is* dangerous. And he just threatened my entire family." He'd said I had friends in high places, but he'd ruin our lives anyway. "I'm mailing you the keys, and then I want nothing to do with you."

"No. I'll be there in the morning to explain."

"You stay away from me, you…*shape-shifter*." I shook a finger at him even though he couldn't see.

"Meri, I'm coming whether you like it or not."

"If you care anything about me, you will leave me the *heck* alone." *Hell. Hell alone! Why can't I say hell?* "You and your creepy low-rent Santa dad need to stay away."

Beau started chuckling.

He's laughing? He's fucking laughing?

My nostrils flared. "I can't *freaking* believe you." *Fucking! Fucking believe.* My mouth just couldn't form the words. "And now I'm having a stroke. Awesome."

"Just stay calm." He chuckled again. "I'll be there as soon as I can."

I was about to yell at him some more, but he ended the call. I dialed back, but it went into the bakery's voicemail.

"Son of a biscuit!" I yelled and then covered my mouth with my hand. *Son of a bitch! Bitch! What's the matter with me?*

My mother appeared in my doorway. "You okay, honey?"

I was far from that. "Do you have any wine?" My parents were not big drinkers, but they usually had the holy grape juice around.

"Sure. But why don't you tell me what's going on?" she said.

"You wouldn't believe me." I scrubbed my face with my hands.

"We could check out my crucifix collection. I have two new editions."

"Fine. I'll talk."

CHAPTER NINETEEN

"You...invited this 'hobo' to live with you?" Dad frowned from the comfort of his leather recliner by the fireplace, sipping his "decaf coffee," which we all knew was spiked with a shot of scotch. He had very few vices, but this was his nightly ritual. Feet up. Fireplace or a good book. One shot. No one cared, but we all pretended not to know. A man needed his secrets, I guessed.

"I think it's very kind," Mom said, sitting next to me on the brown plaid couch, sipping her incredibly tiny glass of red wine. To her left was the big wall of crosses. Over the mantel were photos of the family—my brothers and their wives, their weddings, and all the grandkids. Then there was the sad framed photo of me, all alone in front of a tree.

I looked like such a loser.

I downed my second glass of wine and placed it on the pine coffee table in front of me. "You're both completely missing the point. People literally forget what Beau looks like, and then they fill in the blanks with something else."

"Or," said Dad, "they see what they want to see."

I hadn't thought of that. "What does it mean? Is he some sort of alien who emits a mind-altering gas? And what about his dad? That was beyond aggressive."

"Sounds like a drowning person to me," said Dad.

"Exactly," Mom concurred. "He made all these ridiculous threats, but, baby, he can't ruin us. Or you. Because we don't answer to him." She pointed up to the sky.

Why did she always do that? Just because we were Catholic didn't mean bad things couldn't happen.

"Then why did I feel like…" I lowered my voice, "like he had the power to do exactly what he said?"

"Sweetheart," Mom giggled, "you've always had a bright, wonderful imagination. It's true that we didn't always appreciate it—"

"Especially when she ruined my mower or dug for gold in the pond and destroyed the pump," said my dad.

The mower was one of those things I took apart as a child. Didn't put it back together. End of story. The pond, well, panning for gold was messy.

"I think," said Mom, "that your fascination for mystical, magical things never went away."

They were *not* understanding me. "I don't control what my neighbor sees, and a man can't appear as different things to different people no matter how great my imagination is."

"Welp," my dad bobbed his head, "you are right about that."

I was expecting him to elaborate, but his words were followed by silence. They were not taking this seriously.

"Thanks. You've both been a big help," I scoffed.

"Meri," said Dad, "I can't see gravity, but I know it's there. I know what it does."

"And?" I asked.

"Sometimes you just have to accept that you don't have the answers. But that doesn't mean it's not real."

So was I imagining things? Or were they real? *Make up your minds, people!* "Pfft! You two are zero help," I said.

My mom chuckled. "As if you ever needed anyone's help to figure things out."

෴

The next day, I tried reaching Beau at my place, but it was no use. He was either on his way or he wasn't. Though, he'd have to be completely mad to travel up here to the mountains considering the weather. Snow. Snow. And more snow.

If he had any sense, he'd turn around. Not that I knew how he'd get here. Man didn't have a car. There were no trains or regular buses either.

I headed over to the community center around noon and began helping Libby finish stringing the Christmas lights around the room and across the ceiling. Once the lights were on and the music got going, it would be like the inside of a giant Christmassy gazebo.

"Think anyone will come in this storm?" she asked, looking out the window next to the big Christmas tree by the door. It was decorated with ornaments supplied by the elementary school children. There were sparkly giraffes, ducks, and every animal imaginable made out of bright craft paper.

Is that a glittery poop ornament? Guess the kids were going for the complete zoo look.

"Yes. Absolutely." I began uncasing the red wine. "Snow doesn't stop anyone in this town when free booze is involved." Not that the five thousand residents of our quaint mountain village were lushes, but they did like to party during the holidays. They were also pretty generous when it came to helping one another, and the Holiday Sock and Sip was proof.

"Hey, Libby, we just got the stocking from Rhonda's Travel," said one of our helpers. Most of them were seniors from the high school, who were getting extra credit for their civics class. I knew, because I'd been one of them twelve years ago.

Twelve years. Sigh... Am I really that old?

"Wow, man," Libby crooned. "This is incredible. A week in Greenland." She shoved the envelope back into the stocking.

"Let me see that." I walked over and snatched up the stocking. Inside was a one-week, all-expense-paid trip for two to a spa in Greenland. *My* spa in Greenland. Sleigh ride, reindeer sightseeing, and couple's massage included. The picture on the brochure was of the exact room I'd seen online with the glass windows, in-room jet tub, and king-sized bed.

Oh. My. God. What were the chances?

"Rhonda must be in a generous mood this year," Libby said. "She donated a trip to Walrus World last time. I'll put this one at the top of the display." She climbed the ladder in the corner of the big room and placed the stocking on the hook at the tippy top of the tree-shaped display.

I need that stocking.

As I continued setting up and testing the speakers, I made a promise to myself: I would bid on that trip tonight with the money I'd saved from not splurging on Christmas this year. This trip would be a thirtieth-birthday present to myself.

Funny, I couldn't recall ever buying myself anything like this. I always bought gifts, cooked, and decorated for everyone else. Then I worked all year long to pay for it, year after year. I'd deprived myself of enjoying life. *My* life. That wasn't to say that I hadn't enjoyed my parties or all the fun. I loved every second of giving during the holidays. But maybe it was time to move on and set a different course—find *new* things to enjoy, pursue those bucket list dreams of my own, and push myself out of my comfort zone. I could still love the holidays and explore other things.

I'm getting that trip.

༺ ༻

Around six p.m. the guests began arriving. We'd ended up with way more food than we needed, in my opinion, since Tony's Trattoria provided the catering, and they didn't skimp. Pasta, pizza, salad, and enough bread to feed an army of caroling gremlins.

The DJ played a mix of cheery Christmas classics and modern holiday pop that seemed to please both my parents and the high school students, who kept sneaking wine when they thought no one was looking.

"Libby," I said, finding her by the punch bowl, "keep an eye on the bar, okay? Larry is just putting out glasses and not watching who's taking them." Larry was the designated bartender at most town functions because he charged nothing and only drank a little. Still, those small clear plastic cups were moving fast.

"Sure, Meri. Oh, hey, I wanted to tell you," Libby's words came out slow and dopy, "I'm super grateful you showed up to help. Couldn't have done this without you. Kay is lucky to have you as a best friend, even if you're out there. Yanno?"

"Out there?" I wasn't the one getting high at a charity event.

"I only meant that you've always been a big dreamer." She swayed a bit and then burped. "Don't ever stop, Meri Beri."

Lord. How had this woman given birth to functional adults? It just went to show that everyone had their own destiny despite their upbringing.

"If you want to thank me," I said, "let my parents drive you guys home tonight, okay?" Kay's dad was here somewhere, too, probably goosing the grass like Libby.

"You're right. So right. Can you run the auction tonight?" she asked. "I think I overdid my stress-relief gummies."

No. No... I wanted to bid on my trip. I *needed* that trip. But I couldn't bid if I ran the auction.

My heart sank a little, knowing I'd have to put myself last one more time. "Sure, Libby. Don't worry about it. Just be proud that you put on this great event tonight. And whatever you do, don't drive home."

She gave me a salute and wandered toward the food.

"Meri. Hey..." said a deep voice. For a split second, my stomach fluttered, hoping it might be Beau. Despite not wanting him here, I needed answers. And, maybe, I missed him a little, though I wasn't about to admit it.

I turned to find a man with a big Christmas tree hat staring down at me. He had thin lips and a pockmarked face, and his sweater gave new meaning to the words "ugly sweater." His had the silhouette of a naked woman strategically holding a tiny candy cane. Yes, as in she planned to put it somewhere special.

"Oh, hey," I said, not having a clue who this grotesque creature was, which he picked up on.

"It's me, Kevin from school." He pointed at his chest, poking the lady's boobs on his sweater.

I stared for a long moment before the dots connected. "Kevin Foster?" The guy who gave me the reputation of being a mega-slut?

"So great to see you." His eyes floated down to my breasts.

Gross. "Kevin, I haven't seen you in ages." How unfortunate that he was breaking my winning streak.

"I went away to New York for college. Ended up becoming a lobbyist for a big pharmaceutical."

Also gross. "Well, great to see you," *Grinch of my burgeoning sexual years,* "but I have to check on the eggnog." We didn't have any, but whatever. "Hey, don't forget to bid tonight. Stocking eight has one month of free teletherapy visits."

"Eh, okay. Great to see you, Meri. Maybe we can grab a drink later," Kevin called out as I walked away.

"I'd love that!" I said back. "After I drink rat poison." I looked over my shoulder at his confused face.

Maybe he'd heard me. Maybe not. But there wasn't a chance in snowy hell that I'd give that weasel a second more of my time.

Slutty tumbleweed. Asshole! Did he have any clue what his bullying had done to me? He'd taken a perfectly geeky girl, full of geeky-goodness potential, and shoved her into a shell so deep that she didn't come out until she was twenty years old.

Even now, I had to wonder if my pattern of self-denial wasn't related to feeling so ashamed of myself, like I didn't deserve good things. And for what? For having bad hair? Big boobs? A nerdy obsession with holiday crafting?

Screw that guy. I smoothed my hands over my hair. The mountain air was giving me the frizzies. *Ugh. Not now.* At least I looked spectacular in my tight red dress and white furry coat.

I drew a slow breath and headed to the miniature stage to begin the auction. I turned on the mic and waited for the DJ to wrap up the song "Blue Christmas" by Elvis. As I tapped my foot, my eyes gravitated toward a tall man coming toward me with thick black hair and a long white beard. He stared with intense blue eyes.

I did a double take. "Beau?" The mic slipped from my hand.

CHAPTER TWENTY

"You have to calm down," Beau said as I paced the outside patio of the community center. "Yelling at me won't help."

"I'm not yelling!" I yelled. "I'm demanding! Why is your beard long and white? Why did your dad threaten me? Why are you Black? And Asian? And old and young and invisible? Explain why I feel like I'm going crazy, and make it quick because there's a room of three hundred tipsy people waiting to bid on stockings and take off their socks."

He exhaled. "I'm...I'm..."

"Spit it out!"

He rubbed the back of his neck and let out a growl. "This is going to sound so dumb," he muttered to himself and then looked me in the eyes. "My father is a very famous saint."

That mean jerk is a holy guy? "Bull sheet!" *Bullshit. Bullshit!* "Why can't I say *sheet*? I mean *sheet*." I stomped my foot.

"You mean s-h-i-t?" he spelled out.

"Yes, that!"

"Because a miracle has happened, and now he

wants me to take over for him, which technically makes you…" He paused.

"What?" I snapped.

He came up to me and took my hand. "Meri, the moment I realized what was happening, I wanted to give you space. As much as you needed. Why do you think I tried to keep my distance when you said you wanted to be friends?" He shook his head with an exasperated sigh. "But as much as I want to let this happen at your own pace, I am out of time."

"Time for what?" I yelled.

"Iamthenextsanikus," he mumbled.

"What?"

"Santa Claus," he said quietly and looked away.

"Excuse me?" I frowned, certain my ears were playing tricks.

"I am supposed to take over after my father completes his deliveries on the twenty-fifth."

Wait. Is he trying to say…?

I backed away, the edges of my lips curling. "You think your dad is Santa? And you're next in line for the sleigh?" I doubled over laughing. "You're right. That's dumb!" I slapped my knee.

"Hey. This is your fault!" He pointed a finger at me. "I was fine, living my life and ready to accept that there was no magic inside me, that the change would never happen, all because I didn't believe it was my calling. I mean, how could I? Look at what I did. I was given one chance to run things, and three of our workers died.

"And after searching for ten years for something—*anything*—to inspire me, to help me find my holiday spirit, I came up empty-handed. I gave up. I couldn't eat. Couldn't sleep. I had to take sleeping pills just to close my eyes for an hour. I was losing my mind." His voice grew tender. "Then I met you, and I slept through the entire night on your couch. The more interactions we had, the better I felt, and before I knew it, I began forgiving myself a little, believing in myself a little. But it was your doing, Meri. Meeting you ignited the spark. It *pickled* me off at first, because I'd been determined to do this on my own, but you were right there at the exact moment I needed you."

"Pickled off?"

He shrugged. "Can't swear."

"Beau, stop it right now. You're scaring me."

"Why?"

"Because this is crazy. Santa isn't real. He's a fable."

"Okay. Fine." He put his hands on his waist. "You're right. Your lifetime obsession with Santa means nothing. Definitely not a sign."

My jaw dropped. "I'm not obsessed romantically."

He went on, "And your friends are all going crazy because I'm an alien who emits mind-altering gases. That's what you called me, right?"

I'd said that only to my parents. "You were spying on me?"

"I see everything." He tapped the side of his head. "Comes with the package. So does the fact that people who don't believe find it difficult to see or remember me. And those who do believe see the Santa who connects them to their inner Christmas joy."

Egypt's Christmas joy was a sexy Asian man? Interesting.

No. No. No. This is crazy. "Stop it. I won't stand for these *freaking* lies." *Fucking lies!* "Oh gosh." I covered my mouth and growled. "This non-cussing thing is getting annoying."

"You can't swear because, well, it's naughty," he explained.

"What does that mean?" I yelled. "Why would my ability to curse be impacted?"

He stepped in close, sliding his hand behind my neck. "Because it's done."

I blinked up at him, feeling dizzy. "Done?"

"We're connected through my love. And you can say anything you like, but you love me, too."

"No. No, I don't." I shook my head.

He flashed a big cocky grin. "Yes, yes, you do." He kissed me hard, and his warm mouth and tongue lulled me into a state of bliss. His touch made my chest tingle and made my ski slopes slippery.

"What's happening?" I whispered.

"It seems that despite our stubborn, independent ways, fate has other plans for us."

I blinked at him. This wasn't real.

"Meri, I have to be honest with you, though. I meant what I said. I do love you. You have an amazing heart, you're creative and fun, and you're so darn sexy, you give me a constant North Pole. I can't get enough of you, and I never will. But if this isn't what you want, then you *can* walk away."

"I don't even know what *this* is."

"I don't want to do this without you. I've seen the world and everything it has to offer. What I want is right here." He kissed me again, sending tingles to my toes.

"Beau," I said, "I don't understand what you're asking me to do."

"It's what *I* can do for *you*, Meri. You can be the one woman in the world who truly has a magical life—endless giving, endless Christmas, and endless love."

My heart squeezed with his words, but my mind simply couldn't accept what he was attempting to lay at my feet. "I need a minute. Maybe a few hundred thousand of them." I pointed to the door leading inside. "Also, I have a charity auction to put on."

He smiled, and his face was completely clean shaved now.

I did a double take. "Where did your beard go?"

"You're resisting seeing the truth, but I hope you'll change your mind."

CHAPTER TWENTY-ONE

With hands shaking and knees like bread pudding, I somehow managed to make it halfway through the auction without fumbling or disclosing to the world I was in the midst of a teeny tiny holiday psychosis.

From my spot on the little stage in the corner next to our pyramid of stockings, I couldn't see Beau, but I definitely felt his presence. Or presents?

No, stop it. He is not the next Santa.

Either way, there was a joyous electricity buzzing in the air, and it had my hair frizzing out. The sleek shine of my brown mane was gone, replaced by a straggly mop made of dark ramen noodles.

At least no one seemed to notice. The guests were all smiling and laughing and overbidding on everything.

"Okay. Whoever's under eighteen, look away," I said with a big smile. "Stocking number fifteen is for adults only, donated by our own Buddy's Boudoir." I looked at the card with the description. "Opening bid starts at twenty dollars. Buddy says, and I quote, 'Put the tingle in your jingle this Christmas with our signature peppermint pleasure massage oils.' Gift pack includes a private couple's class on the art of frosting your…" I looked at Buddy to the left of the stage. "I can't say that." I snickered. "But I'm sure everyone can come up with their own ideas."

"I'd like *you* to frost my snowballs!" some man called from the back.

I squinted through the lights. It was that stupid Kevin, and he sounded drunk.

"Sir," I said into the mic with a straight face, "I doubt you have any. But I bet your baby carrot is impressive to all the elves." The room exploded in laughter. "Now, moving on. Can we start the bidding at—"

"Come on now, Slutty Tumbleweed!" Kevin yelled. "Don't be shy! We all know you like to ho, ho, ho."

With my mouth closed, I swept my tongue over the top row of my teeth and sucked my incisor for a moment. Why people did that, I didn't know, but I guessed it was left over from caveman days when your enemy was about to get a bite taken out of his ass.

"You know what, Kevin? You're an acehole." *Asshole! Asshole!* I held up my palm. "I mean *butthole!* Sorry, parents. I know butthole is still a word you don't want to hear at an event like this. But, kids, let this be *my* gift to *you*. Bullies can't be stopped by turning the other cheek, by reasoning with them, or even tattling. The only thing that stops them is speaking the truth. The cold, hard, mean truth. Yes, sometimes, they even need a butt whooping—not that I advocate violence—but darn—some people really deserve it. So, Kevin, here's my truth, which also happens to be *the* truth. You're an insecure little dickins of a man, and you haven't changed since middle school. That's right, ladies and gentlemen, this awesome, oh-so-articulate man ruined five years of my life because I wouldn't let him touch my ti-ti…" I sighed. "My fluffy lady jugs. But, Kevin, I am here to tell you that you have failed at life. You have failed to grow into a man. Because a real man doesn't put people down to make himself feel better."

I drew a long breath, feeling years of nasty, hurtful memories lifting away. *That felt incredible!* I should've done it in middle school.

"You're still a fucking ho, Meri!" Kevin called out. "Ho! Ho! Ho! Bitch."

"Wow." I raised a brow, shaking my head. Some people never learned.

Just then, I spotted my dad pushing through the crowd toward Kevin, my mom hot on his trail. *Oh no. My dad's going to kick the cookies out of Kevin.*

"Oh, guys. No. He's not worth it," I said into the microphone.

There was a tussle and commotion, followed by the back doors flying open. I could see people pouring outside.

Oh shit.

I pushed my way through the guests who were

trying to get outside to watch Kevin learn what kind of hardy stock us Winterses came from. My dad wasn't a violent man, but he was no pussy either. He didn't take crap from people, especially when it came to his wife and kids.

"Dad. Hey! You don't need to do that. He's an idio…" My voice faded as I broke through the crowd, who were all frozen in place, mouths gaped open. My parents were to my side, both with wide eyes.

Kevin was on the ground, cowering in the icy slush, a look of terror on his face. "No. Please don't hurt me," he whimpered.

The creature standing over him had shaggy white fur and long fangs. Its eyes were bright red, and its long, sharp claws were raised, ready to strike.

I stepped back. "What the fork is that?"

"Kevin Foster," said the creature, "you think I don't know what you are? How you treat women? How you fantasize about hurting them? You were a mean little boy, and now you've grown into a sick and evil man."

"I'm sorry. I'm sorry. I'll be good from now on. I promise," Kevin cried and covered his face.

In that moment, I realized that this thing was *his* Santa. A monster.

But why?

The only explanation I could come up with was that he'd grown up without any magical holiday memories, like I had. No singing and fresh cookies.

No hot cocoa and a father who dressed as Santa and delivered gifts. No delicious eggnog and games. No rom-com marathons and sledding in the backyard. His home must have been a nightmare, his Christmases empty and sad if this was his Santa.

"You were given chance after chance, but they meant nothing to you," said the creature. "You are hereby put on the naughty list."

Kevin kept on crying, and oddly enough, I just felt sorry for the guy. He was truly a miserable man because he'd been a miserable little boy.

I walked over and helped Kevin to his feet.

I flashed a dirty look at Beau. "He's probably like this because no one ever showed him kindness or believed in him, Beau. Maybe you'd know something about that."

I blinked, and Beau looked like himself again. No fur. No white beard. Just a guy standing there looking like a big bully.

I walked Kevin to my truck and gave him a ride home.

CHAPTER TWENTY-TWO

I dropped Kevin off, fully aware that he was still a super jerk-faced twat head, but the man needed professional help.

I apologized to him for joking about it earlier. Not very funny. Or kind.

But he promised to see someone for his issues, and I promised I'd try to put in a good word with Santa if he followed through, though he didn't remember anything regarding the monster. He just said that he was sorry for insulting me tonight. And the two thousand other times throughout school.

"It's okay, Kevin. I forgive you." How could I not? I'd had a magical childhood, filled with wonderful memories, family, and one incredible best friend. Sure, there had been hard times, too, but nothing like I imagined Kevin went through. That monster said volumes about what his life had been like.

Kevin hopped out of my truck, and all I could do was wish him the best. If he didn't change his ways, there was no doubt in my mind that he was going to pay for it. Santa was onto him. "Have a merry Christmas, Kevin."

"You too." He wandered into his parents' house, which had no decorations, no lights in the windows, no colorful ribbons on the door. Glum and depressing was an understatement.

I drove to my folks' place with a sad, heavy heart. In the space of a few hours, I'd confronted my childhood nemesis and discovered that his cruel behavior had nothing to do with me. I'd learned that there was such a thing as holiday magic, but that the fantasy was better than reality. The fantasy was safe and comforting, wrapped in years of sweet memories. This new version was frightening and strange. It didn't hold the same joy for me.

I went to my room and took off my coat, ready for a long hot bath.

"Hello, Meri," said a deep voice.

I gasped and turned to find Beau standing there in jeans and his red sweater. "Jelly beans! You scared me. How did you get in here?"

"Comes with the package."

"Oh." I nodded. "Try knocking next time. Did you come for the keys?" I asked.

"I wanted to apologize. I overreacted with Kevin."

"Tell that to the few hundred people you freaked out," I said.

"They won't remember. The beast was only meant for him to see."

I shook my head and took a sobering breath.

"Beau, I don't think this thing between us is going to work out."

"Because of what you saw? It wasn't me, Meri. It was an image Kevin projected onto me."

I sighed. "It's not that. It's..." I struggled to articulate what was milling inside my heart. "Remember when we talked about having restless souls? I thought I'd grown out of all that, but honestly? I think I just put that energy into college, then work and throwing a party every year."

"What are you trying to say?"

"I need to be a hobo for a while—travel, get out in the world, find—"

"But if you choose a life with me, you will do all that," he said.

"You didn't let me finish." I exhaled. "I need to find myself, Beau, not jump into a crazy dream with you."

"So you don't believe it's real?" he asked.

"Oh. I do. I believe in Santa, and I believe in you. But," I paused, "I don't know if I believe in us."

He jerked his head back like he'd just been slapped. "You don't...love me?"

"I actually don't know, but I do know that taking over for your dad is what you're meant to do. I can see you becoming..."

"You can say it. I'm becoming Santa."

I winced. It sounded just too weird. "Yes. That."

"But I don't want to do it without you, Meri, because you might not believe in us, but I do. And I love you. What's the point of spreading joy if I have no one to share mine with?"

I looked down at my feet. "I think that's up to you to figure out." I walked over to my desk drawer and grabbed the gold keys. I walked over to him and kissed his cheek softly. "Say hi to your dad. Tell him not to be such an asshat anymore." My eyes went wide. "I swore!"

Beau nodded defeatedly and took the keys. "I'm going to miss you."

"Merry Christmas, Beau."

"Meri!" my mom called out, knocking on the door.

"Just one sec…" I looked over, and Beau was gone, leaving behind the scent of sugar cookies in my room. *Damn, he forgot to tell me what soap he uses.*

I opened the door and let my mom in.

"Hey, how was the rest of the auction?" I asked, masking the devastation stirring inside. Being with Beau didn't feel right, but neither did ending things.

"Well," Mom said, "after that little turd was tossed out on his keister, Libby finished the rest of the bids, but I don't think anyone was into it much. People just went home after. It was nice of you, by the way, to take pity on that Kevin after he treated you like that."

"That's all you remember?" I asked.

"I remember him being drunk and trying to get in his car. You took control of the situation and got him into your truck." She hugged me unexpectedly. "You're a good apple, Meri."

"Thanks, Mom."

She released me from her arms.

"Oh, hey. I don't think I'm coming back for Christmas." I'd mail them their modest, thoughtful gifts, but I knew I'd need time to digest this new reality.

"But that's your birthday, sweetie. We always celebrate together. Then there's mass and presents and—"

"And I appreciate the work it took to make sure every Christmas felt special. I really mean it. But I think this year I'd like to figure out how to do that for myself."

She stared for a long moment, motherly affection in her eyes. "Well, okay. But we'll be here if you change your mind."

"Thanks, Mom."

"Oh, I almost forgot." She pulled an envelope from her jacket pocket. "Libby said you had the winning bid."

I took the envelope and opened it. "This is the trip to Greenland. But I didn't bid…" I smiled. "Never mind. Thanks, Mom."

"Night, honey. See you in the morning."

I shut my door and hugged the envelope. "Thank you, Santa. It's just what I wanted."

CHAPTER TWENTY-THREE

After my trip home to the mountains, the days flew by.

First, I gave notice at work, telling them I'd be taking my remaining vacation days as planned. So while my last official day would be December 31, I'd turned in my laptop on the twentieth—four days ago.

Next, I gave notice to the landlords and began the task of packing up my stuff. I donated all of the holiday decorations, including the items in my storage locker.

The rest of my belongings—sofa, bed, and kitchen stuff—would all be put into a much, much smaller locker.

Where would I go? What would I do for money after my savings ran dry? I wasn't sure, but something deep inside said it would all work out. I guessed you could say I had faith.

Yes, my friends and family all questioned my very unorthodox decision to blow up a perfectly responsible life, but once I told them I wasn't happy, that I needed more from life, they pretty much backed off. Something about living a life you loved resonated with people. Even the biggest skeptics.

So for the first time ever, I was spending Christmas Eve alone. I'd gone to mass and said a prayer for all the people I loved—and a few I didn't. I had a bottle of wine and one extra-large pizza. I'd watch one of my favorite movies and drift off to sleep, waking up on Christmas morning as a thirty-year-old. No job. Soon to be without a home. A proud hoboess.

I smiled and poured myself a glass of wine before snuggling under my fluffy white throw on the couch.

This is great. I love this. Christmas Eve all to myself. No people to wait on. No cleanup. Yep. This is great.

I turned on the flatscreen and started clicking through my digital movie library.

"Let's see... *Elf? Love Actually? A White Christmas?*" I clicked and toggled, but nothing sounded good.

I set down the remote and sighed. Maybe I just needed more wine.

Or Beau. I got up and peeked out the window, but there were only piles of cardboard boxes next to the dumpster. No red tent. No magical, hot Santa in training who took my entire world and turned it on its head.

Suddenly, my door buzzed.

I sprang to my feet and pushed the intercom button on my kitchen wall. "Hello?"

"Hey! It's Kay."

For one split second, I felt a flicker of disappointment. Then the thought of spending Christmas Eve with my best friend sounded great. I buzzed her in and waited at the front door.

I watched her come up the stairs, carrying a bunch of bags.

"I thought you were supposed to be at your parents' by now?" I said, since we both usually headed home for the holidays.

"Can you believe it? Another freaking storm."

I stepped aside and let her in. "Another one?" I hadn't even paid attention.

"They're supposed to get five feet, and we're getting two." I followed her into the kitchen, where she put her bags down. "Yep. The entire city is snowed in. Airports are closed. Roads are undrivable."

"Really?" How sad. All those people trying to get to family were stuck.

She pulled out two big bottles of tequila. "But the liquor store was open, baby!" She produced some limes from the other bag and then slid out a frozen cheesecake.

"What's that?"

"Duh. It's just a few more hours until your birthday."

"You didn't have to get me a cake," I said.

"Then how about some shrimp cocktail? Or perogies? Spaghetti with meatballs?"

I looked inside her bags. There was nothing else in them. "Those sound good, but if you didn't bring them, it's too late to go shopping. The stores are all closed by now, unless you count the gas station on the corner, but all they have are microwave burritos."

Kay grinned. "I'm having it all delivered."

"From where? Everything's closed."

The door buzzed, and she hit the button. "You'll see."

We both went to my door. I spotted Shawna and her sister, Egypt, coming up, carrying containers of food.

"What are you two doing here?" I asked, both happy and surprised to see them.

"Well," Shawna said, "we were supposed to go to Boston for Christmas, but our flight was cancelled. Kay texted us and invited us over for a potluck."

I looked at Kay, who shrugged. "Well, you always throw a party for everyone. Why not let us throw one for you?"

My eyes teared up. "That is very…" I swallowed hard, "sweet."

"Don't speak too soon," said Shawna. "Because I cooked the casserole myself."

That was huge.

The door buzzed again, and Kay ran to the

kitchen to get it.

Over the next hour, twenty-five more people showed up, including Kay's official boyfriend, Lick, who came despite not celebrating the holiday. Very supportive.

There were also a few people from work, shared friends we'd met over the years, and Kay's sister and hubby. Even Mrs. Larson and Jason stopped by. Everyone brought food.

It wasn't my usual party with the light shows and Christmas-themed snacks. Most of us ended up sitting on the floor or crowded on the couch. But there was music. Everyone drank and laughed. At midnight, Kay lit my cake, and everyone sang "Happy Birthday." It was truly the best Christmas Eve I'd ever had.

But as the evening wound down and people started heading home while it was still safe, I couldn't stop wondering what Beau was doing at this very moment.

Was he helping his dad deliver presents? Was his hair completely white now, and had his six-pack abs turned into a big belly? I couldn't imagine him playing the role, but a part of me didn't want to. I wanted to remember him young, muscular, and filled with kindness he often tried to hide.

Sitting next to Kay, I sighed.

"You okay?" she asked.

"Yeah, I'm just missing Beau. I can't stop thinking what might've happened if I'd said yes."

"Who's Beau?" she asked. "And yes to what?"

I drew a long breath. She didn't remember him. "He was someone I met recently."

"Why didn't you tell me?" She smacked my arm.

I was about to tell her how special he was, but instead told her to never mind. "It would've never worked out."

"Oh, well," she put an arm around me, "you still have time to meet Prince Charming. You're only thirty." She looked at the clock on the wall. "Plus an hour."

I nodded out of politeness, but honestly, I knew I'd never meet another man quite like him.

She added, "You're probably going to meet fifty hot men over the next few months, and they'll all fall in love with you. Then you'll leave, break their hearts, and move on to the next place."

I *was* looking forward to my trip. I'd bought a Eurail Pass and mapped out an itinerary that took me to twenty different countries. I had lists of cheap hotels, museums, churches, and beaches. "It's going to be an adventure, that's for sure."

"Well, just make sure to be safe and check in once a day, like you promised. We need to know where you are at all times," she said.

"I will."

"I'm going to miss you so much." She turned her body and hugged me. "I'm also proud of you for doing this for yourself."

"You're not mad about the cruise?" I asked.

"No! I'm going in July with Lick, and he promised that if anything happened, I'd get to keep the cabin."

"Planning for divorce so soon?" I laughed.

"Actually, I'm planning to ask him to marry me. He's the one, Meri. I know it. But he doesn't think I'm into all that froufrou wedding stuff."

"Really?" I chuckled. Kay was definitely the romantic type who'd always dreamed of meeting the perfect man and riding off into the sunset. "Just make sure I know in advance when the wedding is. I want to be there for every second of it—the dress shopping, the planning, the—"

"Decorating?" She arched a brow.

"Especially that."

"I love you, Meri." She hugged me tight.

"I love you, too, Kay."

"Merry Christmas and happy birthday."

CHAPTER TWENTY-FOUR

One year later...

"Can I be of assistance with anything else, miss?" said the bellhop, who wore a colorful sweater with diamond shapes around the collar.

"No, I'm good. Thank you. I'm just looking forward to a warm bubble bath. Merry Christmas, by the way."

"Same to you, miss."

I locked the door behind him and shed my thick, very worn, red down coat and threw it over the armchair by the fireplace. I clapped my hands together and rubbed them near the flames. I couldn't remember ever feeling this cold, and I grew up in a town that got its fair share of snow.

I kicked off my snow boots, feeling both melancholy and reminiscent. I had left for Europe right after New Year's, only planning to travel for three months tops. After that, I would stay with Kay and look for a new job.

But three months turned into five after I ran into a young Dutch woman on the train to London who had just come from a backpacking trip through Asia. She told me they were looking for English teachers at a school in the Philippines. Free room and board, pay was almost nothing, and I had to get there on my own, but she said it was the best experience of her life. All she had to do was email the director. It took all of ten seconds to say yes. And as luck would have it, there was just enough money in my bank account for a one-way ticket.

Of course, she'd been right. I had the best time teaching what was the equivalent of post-college adults, but they ended up teaching me more than I ever taught them. After two months, my visa was about to expire, so I traveled to Bali and stumbled on work as an English-speaking tour guide. Mostly, I babysat tourists and took them to some of the more secluded beaches.

At that point, I figured I'd been to over thirty countries, and it was time to head home, but as luck would have it, the owner of the tour company asked if I'd be interested in taking a role at a new branch he was opening in Thailand. I didn't know a thing about the country, nor did I speak the language, but that hadn't stopped me yet. *Everything will work out.* So I went, and it was incredible. The food, the history, and the people. Mosquitos? Not so incredible except for their size.

But on month ten, I began missing my family and Kay more than ever. Knowing the holidays were coming made me long for familiar faces, smells, and food.

I flew home right before Halloween and stayed a while with Kay, then my parents. I tried not to think of Beau or all of the things that had happened after we met. It wasn't that I regretted any of it. I only wished that I'd taken the time to "find myself" when I was younger. Maybe then I would have been ready for Beau when he came along, because the one big thing I learned over the past year: there was no such thing as finding yourself.

Life was meant to be a journey where each chapter added to a list of memories you cherished, the things you learned, and the things you lost. Then there were the things you couldn't live without (and *could* live without). But you were never *really* lost. Not in your heart of hearts. You just had more chapters waiting to be written.

Me? I still had many pages left in my story, but I was good with not knowing where everything would lead. I was finally enjoying the journey, and that included taking this trip to Greenland before my voucher expired. I'd just made it with one day to spare.

My family and Kay, who was getting married in April, weren't exactly happy, but I'd be with them for New Year's. And, well, this was my life now. I wasn't going to live it to make anyone else happy. Or unhappy. I could love them and still do my own thing. But one thing hadn't changed. I still *loved* Christmas.

I soaked in the tub until my back, legs, and arms were completely tenderized to a mushy pulp, and then wrapped myself in a white fluffy robe.

I played some Christmas music on my phone and plopped into the big, overstuffed chair facing out across the moonlit, snowy plain before me. In the morning, I'd go and check out the reindeer, though we'd only get a few hours of light.

I leaned back and stared out at the starry night. Somewhere out there was Beau, doing what Santas did. It gave me immense comfort knowing there was real holiday magic in the world, no matter how intimidating or scary it first felt.

As my eyes began to close, a spark of light shot across the sky. I squinted, wondering if it was something other than a shooting star.

Who knew?

"Well, Merry Christmas, Beau," I muttered.

Suddenly that star began changing directions, coming straight toward me. I blinked and then fell from my chair. I blinked again, and it was gone.

I got to my feet, trying to catch my breath. I'd probably imagined it in my half-awake state, but it sure felt real.

I turned to get into bed and spotted a box sitting in the middle of the comforter. It was red with a big white bow.

"Holy sheet." I covered my mouth. *Sheet. I said sheet!* And not on purpose.

I grabbed the box and unwrapped it. Inside was

a note and another box.

To Meri:

May all your wishes come true. Happy birthday.

Love,

Beau

I unwrapped the smaller box and found a gold key. I held it up to the light. It looked just like the ones Beau's dad had left with me.

I held it over my heart. I couldn't lie and say that a day had passed without missing him. Over the last year, I'd seen so many incredible things—temples, mountains, lakes, and the ruins of lost civilizations. I'd met the most amazing, kind people. I'd also seen poverty, death, and cruelty. I'd only experienced a tiny slice of the world, but I finally understood what Beau had said. It needed more happiness. And the only thing *I* really needed, I already had. Love.

I wish to be with you...
Also, seeing some reindeer would be cool.

※

The next morning, I woke up in my bed. It was barely light out, but the clock on the nightstand said it was one o'clock in the afternoon.

I stretched my arms and yawned, feeling a little

disappointed that nothing had happened last night after my wish, but I also felt incredibly excited about being in this gorgeous place. Today was my thirty-first birthday, and I had my entire life in front of me.

What a way to kick it off. "Happy birthday to me."

Suddenly, I noticed a butt pressed against my hip. I slowly turned my head to see a man under the covers, snoring away with his back turned.

"Oh sheet!" I jumped from bed.

"Come back to sleep," he grumbled. "We can have cake later."

"Beau?" I pulled back the covers.

"Meri, please. I'm exhausted," he muttered, pushing up the blanket over his head. "Do you know how hard it is to deliver three billion presents in one night?"

"Beau, what are you doing here? In my bed?"

He slowly rolled over and cracked open his stunning blue eyes. "Just ten more minutes. Okay?"

Oh, no. You are not going back to sleep. I grabbed my pillow and thumped him over the head.

He smiled with his eyes closed. "Now you asked for it." He reached and grabbed my arm, pulling me back into bed.

I was about to protest, but his mouth was on mine faster than I could speak. His tongue delved between my lips, lulling me into a hypnotic state of bliss.

Damn, he still tastes amazing. Like peppermint.

My hands reached for his chest, my fingertips skating over the swells of his pecs and abs and...Oh!

I pulled away. "You don't have any clothes on."

"They were all sooty." He rolled on top of me, beaming into my eyes. "You seem to be missing your clothes, too."

Oh, yeah. "Well, it is my birthday. What better suit?" I grinned.

He returned to kissing me, not at all the drowsy lump I'd seen moments ago. His hands were on my breasts, his mouth was dishing wild kissing, and his hips were snuggling down between my thighs.

"I missed you so much," he whispered.

"I missed you, too."

"Promise you'll never leave again," he added.

I froze for a moment, remembering the night we'd almost...eh-hem, forked. I'd said those same words to him, and it had started a chain of events.

But things were different now. I'd had time to grow as a person and to grow accustomed to who Beau was. More importantly, I'd figured out that love was really the only thing worth finding.

"I will definitely travel again because it's fun, but I will never leave you again," I said, drinking in his handsome face.

His mouth returned to mine, and he thrust inside me. My body exploded with head-to-toe tingles. He moved with me as I rocked my hips, both of us dancing to a rhythm that pumped our bodies with pleasure.

"Oh gosh," I panted. "That feels amazing."

He hooked his arm under my knee, deepening his thrusts. I ran my hands down his muscled back, enjoying the slick, hot penetrating motions of his hard cock. *I mean candy cane! Yes. Yes. So good.*

"Have you been a good girl this year, Meri? Do you want a special present from Santa?" His voice was deep and gravelly.

I stopped and gave him a look.

"Too soon?" he said.

"Please don't ever do the Santa thing again. It's weird."

He laughed and brought his mouth back to mine. I immediately found myself lost again in his taste, his scent, and his heated breaths bathing my neck. His large frame on top of me—chest to chest, hips to hips, and lips to lips—made me feel more than aroused. Nothing else existed apart from our bodies joined, coaxing the most erotic sensations I'd ever experienced.

My toes began to curl, my nipples pearled, and my body locked down, preparing for an explosion.

Oh god! Yes. Yes! Euphoric contractions detonated inside my core, radiating outward through every limb.

Beau made a final thrust and let out a deep, gravelly groan. The room burst with lights of every color, sparkling and swirling while he came. I could hardly see a thing, the brightness nearly blinding me. *That's impressive.*

After a long moment, our panting bodies slick with sweat, he started laughing into the crook of my neck.

"What?" I said.

"Best Christmas present I ever got."

I slapped his arm. "What about me?"

"Best present you ever got, too."

"Hey!"

He rolled off me and propped himself up on one elbow, brushing my frizzy hair back from my face. "Of course you're better than an orgasm. But I'm not sure by how much."

"Beau."

His smug grin melted away, and he kissed me deeply. After a moment, he beamed into my eyes. "Do you have any idea how much I missed you? Thank you for coming back to me."

"Well, you were right. Turns out that I do love you." I cupped his handsome face. "Thank you for not losing faith in me."

"Faith in *us*—a love worth waiting for."

EPILOGUE

"Are you sure about this?" I asked Beau. "I mean, the factory has been running just fine without me for centuries. What's a few more years?"

"Meri, I'm tired of commuting and not having you in my bed every night. And frankly, staying with your parents is a little uncomfortable. Your mom keeps hounding me about if I know Jesus, and they always stare at me like I'm from another planet."

"Well, are you?"

He laughed. "You know I'm not."

He'd tried to explain it once, but it had still boiled down to simply accepting that some things were real, even if we couldn't prove it with a photo or some sort of scientific evidence. Christmas magic was real and, according to Beau, was something you just felt in your heart.

"There's nothing to be nervous about. I promise," Beau said, taking my gloved hand.

"Says the guy who grew up here. To you, this is all normal."

"This is your home now. Our home."

I looked out across the frozen plain. There was nothing for miles and miles in any direction. Beau had spared me the "easy way" to get here because he said it would freak me out initially, so we'd flown to Canada, then to an ice station in Barneo, followed by a helicopter ride. Twenty hours later, here we were.

"Okay. I'm cold. I'm hungry. And obviously you're not going to let me get out of this." I pulled the gold key from my pocket. "What now?"

"Just wish to see your new home."

I shook my head. "This is so silly."

"Meri..." he growled.

"Fine. I wish to see my new home." My eyes began to blur and then refocus. My heart went into overdrive, attempting to comprehend what I was seeing.

I looked at Beau. "You have to be forking kidding me. Is that my dream house?"

He grinned. "It's pretty cool. Right? But check out the rest." He pointed behind us.

I turned, and my jaw dropped. "Oh. My. Gosh. It's beautiful..."

༄ ༅

SANTA SENIOR

"Thank gosh that's all over with. Am I right, Rudolph?"

Ruddy bobbed his antlers.

"Well, it was a good thing we were there to help them along because I was beginning to lose hope that those two would finally accept my gift." It wasn't every day you sacrificed everything—your job, your purpose, and your magic—all so your only son could get out of his own way and find happiness. But I'd been lucky enough to experience the same deep love, and I wanted my only son to experience it, too. For however long he got.

Yes, I missed my wife every single minute of every day, but I knew our time apart wouldn't be forever. And I'd made her a promise to make sure Beau found love.

"I think this one should go right here? What do you say, Ruddy?" I took the snow globe of the factory and placed it between the one containing Meri's hometown and the city where all her friends lived. That way, she'd always feel them close to her.

Rudolph made a little squeak.

"Yes, we'll give them a break from the snowstorms for a while. But they do come in handy."

I sighed contentedly, feeling proud of the work I'd done, but it was time to move on and let my son take over my beloved factory. He was ready—a man now. *Even if he still needs to learn how to laugh properly.* Like a real Santa.

I looked at the wall filled with hundreds of thousands of snow globes. "Where should I go, Ruddy?"

He squeaked and nudged one with his red nose.

"Good choice. Hawaii sounds lovely. The cold here is too much."

THE END

AUTHOR'S NOTE

Happy holidays, everyone! Or if you're reading this at some other time of year, **happy whatever time of year it is!**

I hope you enjoyed this sticky sweet holiday treat! If you read the dedication, you probably figured out that this was the one time I took a request and wrote a story specifically for one person: my Mermexican!

Honestly, he deserves it. After twelve years of cheering me on, making breakfasts, putting on a mermaid tail for my stupid videos, doing book trailers with sock puppets, and always buying me flowers when I complete a book, I could not say no.

BUT! For the rest of my fans, I absolutely kept you in mind while writing this story.

1. Must be different from a regular holiday rom-com.
2. Must have a magical holiday twist.
3. Has to have a happy ever after ending. (No cliffy!)

Check, check, and check!

Seriously, though, I had a ton of fun writing this Christmas story. I've always wanted to do one! Who knows, maybe this will become a habit.

Of course, the best way to let me know if you want more is by **posting reviews, sending me emails, and telling your fellow book-crazed friends about this book!** (Or if you hated it, then cheer for the book you like.)

Don't forget to sign up for NEW RELEASE ALERTS! **You get a FREE ebook when you do!** Head on over to www.mimijean.net or go here: https://bit.ly/3GbbHim

All right. I'm off to finish *Dragon in Boots!* Ohmygod. I just look at the cover and crack up. Mostly because I KNOW the plot twist, and it's HILARIOUS!

Wishing you and your family a very happy holiday season and New Year.

All my love,
Mimi

PS: If you want to hear what I listened to while writing this, check out my playlist on Spotify (or just search for my name): https://bit.ly/3UqUU21

ACKNOWLEDGMENTS

A BIG thank you to all the people who cheer, pitch in, and support each and every book! You know who you are because I've been thanking you for over a decade.

This time around, I HAVE to give a special shout-out to **my readers and ARC team**, who are generally game for anything. Even a Christmas story from an author who writes about weird creatures and throws in the occasional offbeat rom-com or thriller. All you ask for is an entertaining book.

I love you guys!

You make this amazing career possible. Not just for me, but for all the authors you spend your hard-earned money on. In good times and bad, terrible economies and great ones, you're there for us, which makes you the fuel for our engines. So, thank you!

Hugs,
Mimi

ABOUT THE AUTHOR

MIMI JEAN PAMFILOFF is a *New York Times* bestselling author who writes insane plot twists that will have you burning through the pages. Whether it's Romance, Suspense/Thriller, or Fantasy, there are always big heroes to root for, smart and resourceful heroines, and a ton of heart-pumping excitement in every story.

Mimi lives with her extremely patient husband ("Be right there! Just one more page, honey!"), two pirates-in-training (their boys), and their three spunky dragons (really, just very tiny dogs with big attitudes) Snowy, Mini, and Mack, in the vampire-unfriendly state of Arizona.

Sign up for Mimi's mailing list for giveaways and new release news!

STALK MIMI:
www.mimijean.net
pinterest.com/mimijeanromance
instagram.com/mimijeanpamfiloff
facebook.com/MimiJeanPamfiloff